CHICKEE AND THE PAPARAZZI

FURRY UNITED COALITION NEWBIE ACADEMY

C.D. GORRI

ACKNOWLEDGMENTS

Huge THANK YOU to Eve Langlais for letting me write in her super awesome FUCN'A world! I am honored to write for EveL Worlds and can't help fangirling every time I see my name next to our resident mastermind, Ms. Langlais herself! Jersey Sure Shifters have arrived in the Rockies, and they are here to stay.

Happy reading.
del mare alla stella,
C.D. Gorri

FOREWORD

Hello, FUCN'A Readers!

Thank you for downloading my newest FUC Academy tale. I've been a super fan of this world since it began and am hugely honored to write in it for you!

In this story, a formerly soulless tabloid photographer and an ex child reality TV star are tossed together in the deep end and end up on a wild ride full of some unfortunately hairy shenanigans—*FUCN'A style*. Hope you enjoy it!

Happy reading!
Xoxo,
C.D. Gorri

PREFACE

The cacophony of sounds that made up the Big Apple clanged and banged outside the basement apartment building where the meeting was taking place. He looked down at his nametag and grinned at the letter there.

C.

Here, he would only be known by his first initial, not his unfortunate moniker, Clitton R. Russe, Clitt for short. He blessed the day his cousin, Harrison Greymole, sent him everything he needed to know about how to form his own POOP—every evil mastermind needed a *Place of Operations Proper*.

Clitt had the perfect place for his POOP. A secret hidey-hole, just a hop, skip, and a jump away. Okay, fine, it was his grandmother's garage in Jersey City, but all he had to do was take the PATH train to the city, walk a few city blocks past the old churches, skyscrapers, and working peons and tourists, who came to this rat trap and dumped an ungodly amount of money there, to get to his new support group.

Clitt, *er*, C still couldn't believe there was an entire underground network of mad geniuses needing like-minded allies to bounce ideas off of and help with their devious plots to take over the world. These were human bad guys, of course.

No one besides Clitt, *er*, C—at least, not since Wembley Ranklinger had joined, wanted to cure the world of the shifter infestation. It all started when they were children and C had come across Harrison mid-shift during a Greymole and Russe family reunion. Little did young Clitt realize that horrible sight would evermore be ingrained inside his still-developing brain.

Poor cousin Harrison had squealed and jerked. His entire body broke and rebuilt again, sprouting gray, coarse hair that felt rough against C's skin as the mole pushed its way out of his cousin's body. But that wasn't the worst of it. The worst was the pain that lanced through his body when Harrison's sharp teeth attached themselves to his hand, severing his pinky from the knuckle up.

The pain. The blood. The horror. The impossibly gory stump that was all that was left of his pinky!

To this day, C's little stubby was a point of contention at family reunions.

For all you perverts out there, he meant his pinky. Not his other stubby, which was perfectly average, according to his beloved late mother.

Curse you, Bridget McDougal, who'd laughed the first time he showed her his stiffy in tenth grade!

Ahem. Focus.

C was above that kind of thing now. He'd had no girlfriends after Bridget, except for his crush on the star of that ingenious and very exploitive reality series, *Hatched*. How he missed the days of watching as the film crew followed young Chickee Prinz everywhere from the time she was two till she was fifteen.

Oh, he'd had a hard time. Forgiving Chickee from leaving the spotlight was not easy at all for C. But he understood fame was a fickle mistress. People with higher callings, such as he and Chickee, could only do so much in their lifetime. Not everyone had the stamina for it.

As a child, Clitt had been encouraged to forget his cousin's grizzly transformation from boy to beast, but it had never left his mind. Ever since Harrison was sent to jail, the burden of his existence was a little easier to bear. True, he never stopped wondering what it would be like to have those powers for himself. But C understood they were a curse, not a gift.

Fortunately, C was born human. He'd communicated with his cousin infrequently but often enough to know the man was trying to stop the blight that shifters were on the world. Harrison was born cursed with the shifter gene. Poor thing. C had helped him when he could, using his computer prowess to steal identities and send them off to Ranklinger's operation.

Their failure was shocking, but it only helped C conclude he was the only one to fix this problem. At least Harrison was not roaming the streets, lording his genius master over C anymore. Some genius.

Secretly, Clitt could not understand his cousin's desire to be completely, and boringly, human. Being a shifter seemed to have some benefits, but perhaps it was not all it was cracked up to be.

Having to hide what you were all the time? Being at the mercy of your monstrous appetites?

No, that was no way to live. Shifters had to go. Others had come before C with their own hero quests, but each had failed. Just look at Harrison. He'd tried to aid the infamous mad scientist, Wembley Ranklinger, in his quest to cure the world of shifters using their own biology against them. It was too bad that Harrison was being held captive.

No, really, it was.

C could have used a henchman of his own. But that was okay. He didn't need one for his plan to work. His plotting was pure genius in its simplicity. He just had to wait for the right time.

"Order! I call this meeting of Villains Anonymous Group, or as our name badges say, V-A-G, *er*, VAG, to order! Let us start with our creed." The leader of VAG spoke into the microphone attached to the podium.

Every member of VAG stood up, hands over their hearts, C among them. He eagerly squinted his eyes to better read their creed, the very same one he'd found on their website on the black net just a few days ago. This was so freaking awesome!

C was shaking in his boots, size sixes. He'd had to buy them from the little boys' section since his feet were so dang dainty they did not fit into men's shoes yet. He wiped his palm on the butt of his khaki pants and replaced it over his pounding heart.

"I swear to honor VAG,

To keep VAG healthy and clean of impurities,

To fill VAG with the biggest and baddest of villains,

To plug all holes, stop all leaks,

And wipe away that which blights us and our fellow members.

To the VAG brotherhood!"

"To VAG!"

"To VAG!"

"To VAG!" C joined in.

Most of the bad guys there were human, and though Harrison disapproved of him entering VAG, C knew this was the place for him. It was where he got all his inspiration.

Finally, after years of plotting, he had the answer. He would not cure the shifter problem with science and needles—far too messy for a clean boy like him.

Oh no.

Clitt was going to use his VAG connections to expose shifters to the entire world!

"Let's begin," the leader said, snaring C's attention once more. "Does anyone have an evil plot or plan that needs fleshing out? Anything you want to share with the rest of us? L, how about you? No? Okay, well, I tell you what, we will partner up for feedback after everyone shares at least one idea."

Hmm. That was problematic but easy enough to get around. C could not share information with the rest of the human world just yet. He knew what would happen. They would laugh at him then wait for him to say he was joking. When he didn't, they would start looking at him with pity in their eyes.

Oh, how he hated pity! Afterward, they would try to reason with him, asking for proof of the existence of the supernatural, as if these creatures allowed humans to capture raw footage. Shifters were part human, after all. Sneaky little buggers, the lot of them.

Fine, so C had to share his plans. Well, he could make something up, talk about a robbery or heist. Meanwhile, he would sit and collect information. Being in a support group of villains had to have its boons.

C would listen and find an advantage or a tool to use or exploit, and then, he would put his plan into action. Bring the reality of the shifter world into the limelight. Maybe he could even host a reality show that interviewed shifters and followed them around whatever commune, reservation, or prison they wound up in. Maybe he could direct it too!

Just like *Hatched*.

Yes, C would so enjoy that. Perhaps Chickee could co-host with him. Ah! That would be perfect. Yes. Together, they could save the planet.

Let those animals find out just what it means to be cornered. Then C would have his time. His fifteen minutes of fame, though he intended on much longer than that. Who wanted to be famous for just fifteen minutes, anyway?

Yes. This was what he had always wanted. Soon every fold of VAG would know his name! No more initials after his plot went into play. He would claim his scheme as his own, loud and proud, and the name Clitt R. Russe would be hidden no more!

Clitt would go down in history!

Yes. Oh yes, C thought and laughed maniacally, rubbing his hands together as he made plans to turn his dreams into reality.

PROLOGUE

After a long day teaching foundation-blending maneuvers to a bunch of seasoned cadets at the Furry United Coalition's Newbie Academy, Chickee Prinz sighed.

What a day! Who knew her class would be this popular?

She had over 150 students enrolled in what was supposed to be a quiet, small class of about twenty. Of course, Ms. Cooper, the director, had told her there was an intense amount of interest when her name was revealed on the course schedule form, listed as a guest professor.

The class was great, if a little exuberant. One polar bear shifter in particular could not seem to do more than stare every time Chickee tried to call on her. The seven-and-a-half foot tall woman's name was April. Of course, Chickee had only learned that after the bear's friend, Julietta, told her before dragging the star-struck bear out of the room by her oversized foot.

Cluck.

Oh well.

The fact that things like that still happened was cause for some alarm. It had been years since Chickee had been on television, though reruns of *Hatched* had appeared on the interwebs just lately. She supposed it was natural people should still react to her minor celebrity in all sorts of crazy ways. Especially folks in the human world.

Chickee had to admit she'd expected better at FUCN'A. Even so, she would not hold it against anyone. After April left, the rest of the class had been quite tolerable. But two hours of running around like a chicken without a head— forgive the pun—trying to organize her students, give her lecture, and help them with basic makeup applications had been exhausting.

Bok bok. Her inner chicken agreed.

She sank down into the oversized chair behind the desk in the lecture hall where she'd just given a class on makeup and costume techniques used in undercover work to a group of would-be FUCs.

Crazier things have happened, she thought with an amused cluck.

Her inner hen pecked and pawed, trying to turn her human side on to a little shift before dinner. But Chickee was plain worn out. She'd packed up the makeup and other props she'd brought to class with her that day, and all she wanted to do was sit down with a good book and a bowl of Chef Maude's special.

Tom Yum Thursdays featured the renowned chef's special take on Thai food that made certain cadets, and professors, totally salivate for more.

Maybe she could just call *MMM* when she got to her rooms?

Yep. Definitely a plan.

MMM, short for Maude's Meatless Meals to go, was the best darn takeout on campus!

"Long day, huh?" A husky voice intruded on her quiet

time, but the chills said voice left in its wake made her inner hen sit up and listen.

Cluck cluck?

Chickee opened one eye. Usually guarded, the campus at FUCN'A was the one place she'd thought to escape the multitude of fans and relentless media hounds chasing her when her own mother let it slip that the reality show, which had ruined her childhood and almost destroyed her as a person, *Hatched*, might get a reboot next season.

As if.

"Can I help you?"

She closed her eyes, refusing to react to the genuine good looks of the dark-haired, bronze-skinned, handsome-as-sin man standing in front of her.

"Yes, I believe so. My name is Dario Marten. I wanted to introduce myself—"

The name buzzed around her head. She recognized it, for sure. But it'd been a long day, and her brain was kaput. Dario was not that popular a moniker. She'd place him in a minute, she was sure. But honestly, Chickee was more a morning person. It was easier to just let him rattle on.

"Look, I'm headed to dinner. You can talk while I walk," she said, already placing her takeaway order through the new *MMM* app.

She sneaked a glance at Dario, drinking in the fact the male was uber good looking, if a few years younger than Chickee. He had dark hair, tanned skin, a svelte physique, and a debonair kind of style with his linen slacks and vegan leather loafers. The top button of his pale yellow polo shirt was undone, and she approved the smattering of hair she spied.

Manscaping had its place, but Chickee drew the line at chest waxing. No man should have smoother skin than she did if she was considering getting naked with him. Too early for that, but hey, a girl had needs.

If Dario was game, she could tell him which came first—the chicken or the egg. With any luck, it would be the chicken, she thought, covertly checking out his eggs, *er*, package.

"You must get this all the time, but I grew up watching some of your show and I wanted to say—"

"Wait—you said your last name was Marten? Dario Marten. DARIO MARTEN!" Chickee shouted, ignoring the sudden hushes and stares of the people milling about the hallway.

"If you give me one minute to explain—"

"Get away from me you, you *MARTEN*!" She sneered the word like the curse it was.

She could not believe it. A Marten? Here? Of all places! Would that family never leave her alone? Anger and resentment coursed through her as she picked up her pace. Chickee was tapping away on her cell phone, leaving the MMM app and dialing security.

"Ms. Prinz, please allow me a moment of your time to tell you—"

"Yeah, right, buddy."

Chickee paused in her haste to get away from the stupidly handsome, completely unscrupulous bastard. She brought the phone up to her ear, her New Jersey roots ringing in her voice. Her Hudson County accent was always a little more pronounced when her emotions got heightened.

"Security? This is Ms. Prinz. Yeah, I need an escort to Ms. Cooper's office. I'm in the *nawth* hallway. Yeah, I'm waitin'! Bok bok!"

Chickee clucked twice then clicked the end button. This

was crazy. She could not believe it. It was starting all over again. Would these people never leave her alone? Bad enough she had two students freak out on her this week. One of them kept repeating the catchphrase she'd become internationally famous for as a child. "Don't let 'em ruffle your feathers."

If only the public knew how apt that was. Chickee was a hen shifter. A pure white Jersey Giant hen, to be exact. She'd been put up for adoption at birth and never knew her biological parents. The woman who'd taken her in was human and didn't know what Chickee was until she spontaneously shifted on her thirteenth birthday.

By then, it was too late. Genevieve Prinz, her adoptive mother, had sold the rights to her story and had created the media feeding frenzy around Chickee's life, starting when she was just a toddler. *Hatched* got its name from her mom, who'd said adopting her daughter was "the best scheme I ever hatched." Of course, she had no idea Chickee was a shifter at the time of her adoption.

Bok bok.

Yes, Genevieve claimed to love her, but Chickee had never forgiven her for taking away her childhood. Or for abandoning her after she'd started shifting. The human woman was wholly unprepared for that event, but Chickee had to hand it to her. At least, she did not tell.

The fact she'd thought about it was one of the most shameful facts of Chickee's life. It had taken one very ornery crocodile shifter and his enormous fox mate to change Genevieve's mind.

How could she do that to me?

But it was not a far leap from one nightmare to the next, Chickee supposed. After all, Mommy Dearest had lined her own pockets while Chickee was raised by producers, cameramen, and wardrobe people while every moment of her life was portrayed on television.

Sound fun? Well, it wasn't. Not at all. In fact, *Hatched* had been a nightmare of a life. After she had her first shift, Chickee had to work doubly hard to keep her secret. Her mom had slowly started a downward spiral toward alcoholism and denial. Once Genevieve had it in her brain to tell the world her daughter was an actual chicken, Chickee knew she had to do something.

She'd needed help. While scrolling the dark web for hints, she had stumbled on and later met with Viktor Smith, a FUC agent, who had helped her get in touch with the right lawyer to work on her emancipation. Of course, that was after he and his mate had visited Genevieve Prinz with a series of ultimatums.

Chickee wished she cared, but truthfully, she had no feelings for the woman who'd adopted her other than regret. She tried to find her real family or flock, but it was impossible. No one knew where she came from.

Once her emancipation was granted, Chickee left the U.S. and fled to Canada, where she could attend school like a normal girl. Chickee had bowed out of the limelight forever. Or so she hoped. Her dream now was to become an agent. Just like the man who'd saved her from all the attention and confusion that had consumed her adolescence.

Viktor and his mate, Renee, helped her in so many ways and were still good friends. He'd even suggested this gig at the Academy teaching makeup and disguise skills—things Chickee excelled at, for obvious reasons. But here was Dario Marten, trying to mess it all up for her!

No.

Absolutely not.

This hen was not about to get plucked by some weasel in nice clothing.

"Did you just call security on me? I'm an agent, Ms. Prinz. You know what that means, right? I am on the same side as you!" he stated, seemingly astounded.

"All I know is you are following me, like your unscrupulous father did for my entire life, Mr. Marten. Do you people have no shame?" Chickee asked, pushing her short, blonde hair behind her ears.

"Ms. Prinz, I am not working for my father's paper any longer. I just said I'm an agent—"

"Photographers from *The World According to Marten* have been hounding me for years. There is no way I believe you. Besides, coincidence or not, I will not work anywhere you or your family have any influence. Excuse me. Officer?"

"Did you call for security, miss?"

"Yes, I did. I need to see Ms. Cooper now," she said, straightening her shoulders.

Without looking at Dario, Chickee tossed her scarf over her head and hustled behind the confused-looking security officer. She did not care what the weasel behind her did, follow or not. Chickee was on a mission, and she needed to have a meeting with Director Cooper.

Right now.

Contract or not, Chickee Prinz was not about to stick around to get screwed by another Marten. And, no, she did not mean in the fun, smexy-times way.

Cluck cluck?

No, she snapped at her inner horn-bird.

This was not the time to get all googly-eyed over some tall, dark, sexy-as-all-get-out-but-completely-unattainable man. Besides, she should never allow her guard down around a Marten! His family was evil.

Fine. Maybe not evil. But they were the worst kind of paparazzi scum she had ever encountered. There were dozens of tall, strapping males inside the Marten family group. Those tayra males had disguised themselves as everything from coaches and teachers to nurses, doctors, and even fellow students to get the inside scoop on Chickee when she was a kid.

She was so not doing this. Typically, if there was a Marten around, Chickee would flee. But was she really going to give up another dream because of one unscrupulous little weasel?

That was the real question.

1

Dario Marten walked into his home FUC office casually. He was wearing his usual casual linen slacks and a polo shirt. Summer in Canada was surprisingly warm, not like LA warm but still hot enough to warrant the large double caffeine, nondairy, mochachoccalattiato from the new *Quackbanks Coffee* drive-thru a few streets away.

Casual office day. Casual attire. Casual mood.

At $6.85 for the sweet and frothy concoction, Dario was determined to enjoy every last drop, despite the annoyed growls and dirty looks from his peers. He ignored every last one of their narrow-eyed stares and chesty growls.

Jealous. All of them. And why wouldn't they be? The caffeine-loaded chocolatey goodness was undeniably good.

Slurp slurp slurp.

Now a bona fide FUC agent, Dario had to admit life had certainly taken some unexpected turns. So, he'd recently blown his cover on a secret ops mission to gather intel on a new crime boss who seemed intent on dealing in shifter identities.

Picking up where the U.S.- based PRICs—that's *Private*

Resourceful Investigative Contractors—who'd been working the case left off, Dario thought, cutting to the chase to uncover the new head honcho's identity might be worth it. Of course, his threats ended up getting him busted, and an official complaint had been filed, unofficially of course, since the humans knew nothing about the Furry United Coalition.

"Get in here, Marten!" bellowed Chase Brownsmith, FUC agent and ferocious bear shifter.

"Yeah, boss. Be right there. Almost done," he replied, slurping loudly.

"I said NOWWWW!"

Ooofa.

That bear sure knew how to roar. Even from across the office, he managed to get spittle on Dario's skin.

Dario retrieved a handkerchief from his pocket and wiped the spittle the giant male left behind on his forehead. Some shifters had more brawn than others, and Dario knew better than to further agitate the man.

"You really screwed this up, didn't ya, kid?" he grunted, slamming the file on his desk as Dario sat down gingerly.

"Well, I guess that depends on your outlook, sir."

"My outlook? You were supposed to be undercover as a widower, whose wife disappeared under mysterious circumstances, looking for a new life. You walked in there dressed like an elderly candidate for the retirement home, Marten! Not exactly screaming playboy who murdered his wife, now, were you? What is wrong with you?"

"They said widower! My brain equated that to old man," he tried to explain. "I'm sure I can salvage—"

"No. You will not be salvaging a thing. I have two agents in the HOLE because of you."

"Well, really, it was just dumb luck Dr. Finn was nearby

to set up that *Home Office for Life-Threatening Emergencies* right away. I am sure Margot and Carl will heal up just fine—"

"Yes. Because of Dr. Finn. Not you, Marten. Now, this is your last chance. I voted for you to get gone, but Miranda told me to try for patience. So, this is me having patience with you," the bear said through gritted teeth.

The temperature in the room had already shot up at least ten degrees, and it seemed the more annoyed Chase got, the warmer it became. Dario closed his lips. He really had to stop egging the man on, but he could not help himself. His family was known for being impossible.

It was why they were so good at getting the dirt on people who did not want their dirty laundry aired publicly. Tayras were tenacious little critters. No match for bears physically, but Dario was cunning and smart. His mind was already racing with possible outcomes of his last unfortunate mission.

Would they send him on a fact-finding mission in Alaska? Have him keep tabs on that infamous tiger mafia family in Siberia? The possibilities loomed, but Dario had to admit shock when Chase spoke next.

"I am sending you back to school."

"Um. What?"

"You heard me, Marten."

"My name is Dario. Marten is my last name. It is just confusing when you use it like that, reminds me of Little League. I had the most obnoxious coach who insisted on calling me by my last name. Brings back terrors," he muttered, looking away when the bear shifter's growling grew deeper and louder.

Freaking bears. They had no couth as far as Dario was concerned. Big bullies, the lot of them.

"You're going to take some refresher courses at the Furry United Newbie Academy. Brush up on some skills. Here's the FUCN'A schedule. Now. Get. Out."

"But, sir, I don't think I need—"

"GET. OUT!"

"Fine. Want a sip before I toss it?" Dario asked, standing up and swirling the half-inch of brown liquid left in his to-go cup.

Brownsmith grabbed the plastic container and flung it into the garbage, growling all the while.

"Hey, Dario!" Miranda Brownsmith called after him, and he stopped short, giving the bunny shifter a sweet smile.

"Yes, my love. Tell me, are you ready to get rid of that one yet?" he teased.

"Stop it before my mate eats you," she chided, handing him a stack of files. "I wanted to ask you to check out these various leads we've received about an underground plot to reveal the shifter secret."

"Do these have anything to do with *The World According to Marten*? I told you before, Mrs. Brownsmith, I have nothing to do with my family's business anymore—"

"I know you said that, but if you could just—"

"Apologies, Miranda. I have been directed to take some refresher courses at FUCN'A. Maybe someone else can look into these for you," Dario replied politely.

He ignored the bunny's probing gaze and walked outside. Seated inside the nondescript sedan he drove, Dario gazed at the schedule of classes Brownsmith had handed him before he'd left the bear's office. A familiar name on the roster of professors stood out among the others, and Dario paused.

"Can it really be her?" he mused aloud.

Chickee Prinz. Her name was a blast from the past Dario

was not prepared for. He vaguely remembered the years *Hatched* was on air. Hell, how could he not? His father had been completely obsessed with them printing every single detail about the young reality star's life in his tabloid.

This was exactly the kind of distraction Dario needed from the unfortunate turn his last investigation had taken. Maybe Brownsmith's idea to return to FUCN'A was not so bad. After all, maybe Dario could finally make amends to the woman whose life was made hell by the soulless photographers and sleazy paparazzi his father had sent to hound her day and night during the height of her fame and for years after.

Yes! Dario could apologize for his unscrupulous father's tactics. Then maybe he could find the focus needed to make better decisions for his career—before he ruined it.

Of course, once he'd settled into his temporary accommodations and taken a few classes, a week had passed before Dario ran into the sexy little chickadee. He sure as cluck was not prepared for the jolt his inner tayra felt when he walked into her classroom and spied the sexy little female, leaning back in her chair with her eyes closed.

Hot damn!

The Chickee he remembered had gone from a skinny little child with a flat chest, frizzy hair, a face full of freckles, and a mouth full of metal to a too-thin, heavy-eyeliner-wearing angry young woman who'd admittedly made Dario's teenaged heart race. He could see her now, sitting on the witness stand, pointing her black-nail-polished finger, and accusing his father of ruining her life in the televised court case where she sued her mother and the producers of *Hatched* for legal emancipation.

She wasn't wrong. Dario's dad was a total dirtbag. He and Dario's seventeen half-brothers were the reason Dario had left home to begin with. In the wild, tayras were solitary creatures, but the shifter species was a little different. The men bedded several females for the sake of propagating the species. Fact was, they bred like bunnies, and tayra males, like his dad, raised their male offspring without their female counterparts.

The only thing that stopped Dario's kin from being labeled womanizers was the fact the females of his kind seemed to not only accept this behavior but they actually encouraged it. The women lived in apartment or condominium complexes close to cities. They ran their own businesses, enjoyed the arts, had one helluva lifestyle.

Dario just did not understand why they could not do it with their men. And his father and brothers could not understand why he wanted to rock the boat.

"I swear you would have made a better human, Darito," his father complained often and loudly.

And there it was. The biggest gibe of his life. His father thought him weak. Always had. And all because Dario refused to hook up on those little *procreation exploration weekends* his kind seemed perfectly fine with. The whole thing just skeeved him out. He'd called his mother once to ask if she thought of him at all, and the woman laughed.

Why would she? He was being raised as a true tayra male and she got to live in a beautiful Manhattan apartment owned by *The World According to Marten Press* with several of her friends and Dario's two sisters.

No. Dario did not understand relationships. He did not get women. But he thought he knew right from wrong. Fact was his father had wronged Chickee Prinz. Like it or not, he was going to apologize for his family. Someone had to.

Grrrrr.

His tayra growled and barked inside him. The smallish,

tubular mammal was an ornery fucker most of the time, but he hated it when Dario made him talk to others.

We have to do this, for ourselves as much as for her, he tried convincing the creature.

Mind made up, Dario entered the classroom where the daily schedule said she would have just finished her class called *The Foundations of Foundation: A Guide to Making Makeup Work For You*. Interesting. He wondered if she had a book on it since it was his use of the wrong shade of tan that had outed his elderly widower disguise. That and the fact he was supposed to have killed his wife and was looking for a new identity, which would have led to him unveiling the new baddie who was dealing in stolen identities—*shifter ones*.

Okay, so Dario needed some help. Maybe this apology could work for both of them. He could offer her some closure, and she could give him some pointers.

Win win.

Only problem was the polished woman sitting in the professor's chair differed vastly from Dario's memories of her. This Chickee Prinz was all grown up, and the truth was she was stunning.

Even from here, Dario could make out full, ripe breasts tapering to a tiny, indented waist. He could not see the flare of her hips, but he just knew the female had a perfect hour-glass figure. Her sandy-blonde hair was stylishly cut. Her face dusted tastefully with minimal makeup, just meant to enhance her features, like that cute little button nose and her delightfully plump lips.

Sniff sniff.

Dario could not help scenting the air surrounding her. She smelled like peaches and wine, gummy candy, and Jell-O shots. Sweet with a punch that hit him right in the gut.

The result was a lightning bolt to his senses. It'd been quite a while since his tayra was even remotely interested in scoring a little female one-on-one time. Maybe the flame of his youthful crush could be rekindled to an adult-like inferno.

Of course, the second he opened his mouth and told the delectable little nugget his name, the poop hit the fan.

"Wait—Dario? As in *Marten*? Dario Marten!" Chickee shouted.

"Wait a second!" he said the second his brain caught up with the fact she was running away.

"Security? This is Ms. Prinz. Yes, I need an escort to Ms. Cooper's office. I'm in the south hallway. Yep."

"Did you just call security on me? I'm an agent, Ms. Prinz. You do know what that means?" He tried to reason with her.

"All I know is you are following me, like your unscrupulous father did for my entire life, Mr. Marten. Do you people have no shame?"

For the life of him, Dario had no response. Sure, he had shame, his father the biggest shame of all, but he was not about to air his laundry in front of the entire WANC.

"Come with us, sir," a security officer said, and Dario followed, head down.

Maybe his father was right. His kind rarely went around apologizing to women. He could only imagine the old man's words if he could see him now.

Dario really made a lousy tayra shifter.

Bark. Yowl. Click.

2

"Let me get this straight," Alyce Cooper, the director of the Furry United Coalition Newbie Academy and black llama shifter, began. "Ms. Prinz, when you were a reality television star, Mr. Marten's family-owned tabloid made your life a personal hell? Is that your claim?"

"It's the truth."

"As a Marten, I have to say that is libelous and mostly false," Dario murmured.

"Ha! How would you know?"

"Of course, I would know. I was there, watching *Hatched* with the rest of the world. That show made your life hell, Ms. Prinz, not my father—"

"Oh, really? Then I suppose you know Marten Press was the biggest producer of *Hatched*? That Gabriel Marten arranged for members of your family to infiltrate my school, show up at parties, clubs, high school football games, dressed as students? Did you know your cousin Maurice was my first kiss? It was all staged, and I was humiliated when he admitted it during an exclusive interview in *The World According to Marten*!"

"That cannot be true," Dario said, but he looked uncertain, and the scent of his surprise filled her nostrils.

Bok bok.

"Well, it is true. He even used a different company to hide the fact he was staging every nuance of my life and making money from it at every turn. I never said your father wasn't smart. The production company was listed as *MPM Live*, but it was just a shell, a dummy corp, created solely to keep the fact that the very same tabloid that sent paparazzi to hound me from the age of three on had set me up for every damn take! Your father stole moments of my life from me, Mr. Marten!" Chickee shouted.

"That bastard," mumbled Dario, looking shocked and appalled.

Well, that was surprising. Dario seemed just as furious with his father as she was.

"I never knew you were a shifter, and I admit it was a shock to see your name on the roster here. Ms. Prinz, I did not know my father did any of that to you. As you can imagine, I was a child, myself—"

"Yeah, well, he used children my age, your family members, to trick me," she said, anger making tears well in her eyes.

Crap. She hated crying. But this was too much. Chickee might never fulfill her dream of becoming a FUC agent, but she did not have to revisit this particular hell for the sake of one greedy media mogul's weaselly son.

"I demand he be kicked off campus," Chickee said, slightly deflated after witnessing a Marten have a decidedly human moment.

Could it be this apple fell a bit farther from the ol' family tree? No. She could not afford to think like that. Not when she was so close to fulfilling her dreams of being a veritable FUC agent.

"Ms. Prinz, I understand you are upset, but kicking Dario out of the Academy is not an easy decision for someone in my position to make," Ms. Cooper stated.

"Kick me out? On what grounds? That she doesn't like my dad? That is absurd. I am an excellent FUC!"

"Wait a minute." Ms. Cooper tried to interrupt.

"First, calling yourself an excellent FUC is ludicrous. Second, you think I don't like him? Oh no, don't be mistaken, Mr. Marten. I *loathe* your father. He is totally unscrupulous, uncaring, and devoid of all sense of a moral compass! That man is a, *er*, weasel! Ha!"

"He is a tayra, not a weasel. Though I understand your confusion. Both creatures are mustelids, but please, Ms. Prinz, do not just lump us all together," Dario Marten said, his accent thickening with his anger.

Was it wrong she found the deep rumble sexy? Probably. Or the slight lilt and the way the cadence of his words changed in his heightened emotional state? Definitely. Chickee could not afford to be swayed by his innate prowess.

So, she'd almost forgotten the Marten family hailed from Quito originally. It explained his tan skin, impossibly dark eyes, and thick, glossy hair—a testament to his ancestors. Quito was in Ecuador, and that was in South America, and that explained Dario's accent—but not why she was suddenly infatuated with him, *er*, it.

She'd visited there before. Quito was a lovely town in Ecuador. Chickee had once tried to get away from her insane life by fleeing to the South American city. The flashing cameras and rabid reporters had gotten to be too much, so she'd literally opened a map and pointed. Quito it was. But when Chickee's plane landed, it was to discover Ecuador was the one place that held more damn Martens than LA and New York City combined.

Sad cluck.

"Hold on a minute, people. I think if you just allow me to explain the circumstances—" Ms. Cooper interrupted again, but Dario beat her to the punch.

"Ms. Prinz, I do not speak for my father, but I am whole-heartedly sorry for any discomfort you experienced at his hands. I think, if you look at this objectively, you might find you were not the only collateral damage from my father's ambition."

Dario turned his unwavering gaze on Chickee, and she became locked in that impenetrable stare. His voice, so deep and easy, smooth as silk, was comforting. He was telling the truth about his father, and it made sense. He was not responsible— Wait. What?

That weasel!

"I think, Ms. Cooper, you will find, if you look at my file, that I am dedicated to FUC. It is my life now. I have no connection to my father, and since I am five years younger than Ms. Prinz, I could not have possibly had a hand in the events she so rightly sued Marten Press for," he continued.

Chickee growled. This was how people like him got others to trust them! He thought he could just flash his big brown eyes and give her a sexy grin and she would forget her entire life?

Cluck you!

So what if the man was good at his job? A job she wanted, she admitted, if only to herself. Working as an undercover FUC agent was Chickee's biggest dream, but her celebrity status made it impossible. Teaching was as close as she could get to the real action.

She'd come to the Academy to give lessons on makeup and disguise to help shifters who actually had a shot at being agents. Her unfortunate childhood had basically destroyed her dreams. She'd thought it was all behind her now, but here was another sleazy Marten, trying to dredge up all the muck instead of leaving it where it belonged— dead and buried!

Ugh. That entire family was like a canker sore, popping up at the most inopportune time, marring her, and making it impossible to go unnoticed. Just like a weasel to mess things up.

"Again, I would like to extend my most sincere apologies to Ms. Prinz for any offense at my family's hands. But at the risk of repeating myself, that was a long time ago, and I was neither responsible nor complicit in any of the actions taken by my father's business against Ms. Prinz," Dario said, flashing his million-dollar, panty-wetting grin at Ms. Cooper.

Really? Chickee scoffed. Did he think his cheesy playboy smile was going to buy her forgiveness?

"Your family ruined my life, Mr. Marten," Chickee growled. "And now, you are here to take what little I have managed to get back for myself!"

"That is not true," he said, and for a moment, the hurt in his dark brown gaze seemed real.

Chickee shook her head. She refused to be taken in by his false sincerity. Hadn't she seen it all before when she'd taken his father to court at the ripe old age of fifteen in an effort to stop the incessant hounding by the photographers and reporters in his employ?

Dario was still talking to Ms. Cooper, but Chickee was far away from them both. Memories rushed through her brain, and Chickee closed her eyes against them.

Camera flashes in her face. The sound of fans screaming. The private facts of her life printed in bold across countless social media accounts and cheesy tabloid magazines. Her mother admitting she sold her adopted daughter's privacy to pay for her own extravagant lifestyle.

Dario's voice interrupted Chickee's trip down nightmare lane. The weasel actually looked to be winning Ms. Cooper over.

Heck. To. The. No.

"Ms. Prinz's life had already been turned upside down by the reality show *her mother* had created for her. I do not know how difficult being in the spotlight was for her, but I recall episodes of *Hatched* where Ms. Prinz was invited to speak as a guest at certain awards and events. She tossed the ball out at the Yankee Stadium during that big charity game to benefit the homeless. She attended various concerts, had cameos in countless films and TV shows, and even had a song written about her by a famous rock band."

"Oh yes, I remember that," Ms. Cooper replied with a small smile.

"Are you serious?" Chickee hissed.

"I am not making any judgment calls, Ms. Prinz. That is not my job. But, while I understand you're upset, and the fragile emotional state you are experiencing might have been caused by that trauma inflicted by your own mother's complicity in creating *Hatched*, it should have no impact on my career. Perhaps therapy would be a good course of action for the two of you? As for me, I've been a FUC agent for five years, and as requested by my superiors, I am back at FUCN'A to brush up on some skills required for my sensitive undercover work. I have no design to hurt or bring attention to Ms. Prinz—"

"Oh please! Like you need to work, Mr. Marten! And

FYI, I broke all contact with my adopted mother the second the judge allowed my emancipation. I know exactly who hurt me, and your family was part of that," Chickee hissed. "Pretend all you want to that you had nothing to do with it, but we all know your father is a billionaire with no scruples. Now, if I might I remind you, Ms. Cooper, my contract states I will be protected from all forms of media frenzy—"

"Really? I seem to recall you liking the attention, Ms. Prinz," Dario snarled.

"Did it seem that way when I was being followed every waking moment of my life? Huh? Did it seem like I was having fun when I was damn near trampled by your father's men when I was trying out for cheer team? Or how about my first school dance? The driving test I failed because I was run off the road by his henchmen. Did any of that seem like I liked it?!" Chickee screeched.

Chests heaving, panting for air, her temperature nearing inferno level, Chickee faced off, toe to toe, with Dario Marten. Irrational? Maybe. But that weasel ruffled her feathers in the worst possible way! Flippant and arrogant— that's what he was! How dare he claim to know her?

"Enough!" Ms. Cooper bellowed. "Listen up, you two. I called you here for a reason, and it was not to referee this, well, whatever the FUC this is!"

Chickee frowned, did Cooper call her there or did she ask to see Cooper? Whatever. It was probably not a good time to argue that point.

She watched Dario's eyes narrow, and they both paused their tirades and turned to face the director. Odd to find herself standing beside her nemesis in solidarity.

Something was rotten in Director Cooper's Office, she thought—referencing her favorite Shakespeare play—and Chickee wanted to know what it was.

"Well, why are we here, then?" Chickee asked.

"Yeah, I thought Ms. Prinz was trying to get me kicked out of FUCN'A," the weasel with the sexy voice remarked.

"I am," Chickee whispered to him.

"What? That is completely unreasonable. This is my career—"

"And that was my life—"

"For FUC's sake! Do I need to separate you two?" Ms. Cooper stood and slammed her hands on her desk.

"You take that chair," she growled at Chickee.

No fool, Chickee knew when to back down. With a short cluck, she dropped her featherless bottom into the surprisingly soft seat and waited.

"And, you, take that one," Ms. Cooper grunted, directing her next command at Dario.

The weasel walked unhurriedly to the seat beside Chickee, sparing her a short, and somewhat haughty, glance as he eased down with a finesse and grace no man should have.

Wormy little weasel.

"Now, the Furry United Coalition needs your help, but it will require the two of you to work as a team. Recent intel suggests there is a new player in the identity theft case we handled a few months ago with a couple of PRICs from New Jersey. You might recall the case—"

"You mean the case where *Private Resourceful Investigative Consultants* Tony Leeds and Sergio Gravino found the culprits responsible for kidnapping Tony's adoptive sister, Julietta DiCarlo, Dr. Damon Finn's mate? Yes, I know the case," Dario replied, sitting up.

"Shut up, Captain Interruptus," she growled.

"Children, if I have to separate you two again, I promise

you will not get any dessert for a week," Alyce Cooper snarked and rolled her eyes.

Oooh. This must be big, Chickee thought, licking her lips. She'd heard of PRIC, of course. Ever since she discovered she was a shifter, Chickee did her best to keep abreast of the goings-on of the secret world that existed parallel to the human world.

She'd spent the years since her emancipation learning what she was, where she actually came from, and trying to build a life apart from her childhood hell. Some things could not be undone, but that didn't mean she should ever stop trying to live her best life. Even her inner chicken agreed.

Cluck cluck.

"So, you two, together, undercover. Do you think you can do that?"

"Wait, you mean I'll be working as an agent? Not an instructor?" Chickee asked Ms. Cooper.

Holy. Shit.

This was it. Her big break. She needed this *sooooooo* badly.

"For this assignment, yes, Ms. Prinz. This would be your first foray into undercover work, but I need to know you two can pull off working together before I okay it. Nothing is more important than keeping our secret. Do you understand?"

Chickee licked her lips again, a nervous habit she'd developed as a kid when she first understood it was not normal to have cameras and microphones in her face at all times. The first time she understood her life was different was when she couldn't play with this little girl at a local park because the girl's mother didn't want to sign a release for her image to be used in the show. That sort of thing happened a lot afterward. Each time, it made her feel freakish and alone.

Chickee had been heartbroken. She never developed the regular relationships children did as part of their growth. Sparing a glance toward Dario, she swallowed audibly. His too-handsome face was ridiculously unfair. Ms. Cooper was going on about their assignments, and Chickee was only half listening, but one word tripped her up.

"Wait. We have to pretend to be dating?"

"Yes. Think you two can do that?"

Chickee's eyes widened. Well, if she had to work with a fake boyfriend, she could do worse than a good looking FUC. At the very least, Chickee would enjoy the view. She nodded her head, earning her a confused glare from the man.

"You're okay with this?" Dario asked stupidly.

Was he a moron? Of course, she was okay with this. Didn't he see this was her big chance?

"Say yes, idiot," she grumbled.

"Um, Ms. Cooper, what are the details? What exactly would the assignment entail?" he asked, and Chickee could have kicked him.

Didn't he know she wanted this more than anything? He arched one perfect eyebrow at her and waited for the director to speak.

"You two will pretend to be in a deep, committed relationship. You will travel to New York and then go through the Holland Tunnel to stay at Stein Luxury Resorts Hotel in Secaucus, New Jersey. Once there, you will pick up an envelope from the front desk containing two tickets to the CANS."

"The CANS? That's this Friday," Dario said.

"Yes. We have received alarming news. There've been

whispers that an attempt to reveal the shifter secret will take place at the CANS this year. You will be our eyes and ears on the ground."

"You mean the Cannes Film Festival?" Chickee asked.

"No," Dario muttered, and his frown deepened. "She means the *Characters, Actors, & Notorious Stars* awards."

"I've never heard of it," she replied with a frown.

"This is only the third ceremony," he mumbled.

"I see. So, it's an annual thing? Who organizes it?"

"The CANS were started by Marten Press," Dario confessed, and his cheeks turned ruddy.

At least he has the good sense to look ashamed, she thought, as her blood ran cold.

"Well, that figures," Chickee replied and snorted with derision.

"May I continue? Traveling as a couple, you will attend the ceremony where you, Ms. Prinz, have been invited as a guest announcer—"

"What?!"

"Mr. Marten's father has agreed to work with us."

"My father would never agree to such a thing unless he was being threatened."

"The council suggested he cooperate," Ms. Cooper informed them.

"Makes sense," Dario muttered.

"So, we're attending the CANS to unveil the unknown culprit behind an attempt to reveal the existence of shifter kind, and we're going to squash any possibility of that secret leaking into the human world. Sound right?" Chickee asked, mind racing with implications.

"You're forgetting something. We hate each other. I mean, why even take me? He can just go to the ceremony and ask his father for help."

"I could, except I am not invited, Ms. Prinz. I have not spoken to my father since I left his company and became a FUC agent," Dario said between clenched teeth.

Chickee's heart was pounding double time inside her chest. How could this be her chance? Her one opportunity to become a real-life FUC agent, and she needed *him*, of all people.

"Mr. Marten's father agreed to this on one condition. You. He will only allow Dario on site if you are there with him and if you promise to act as one of the CANS announcers," Ms. Cooper said, allowing that gem to sink in a moment.

"Why does he want Dario?" she asked.

"Because my father wants me back in the fold, Ms. Prinz. He will do anything to lure me back to the family business. He thinks if I see the glitz and drama of the CANS, I will leave FUC."

"Will you?" Chickee asked, and Dario tilted his head, as if deep in thought.

"No. I left all that a long time ago."

"Well, now that's settled. Ms. Prinz? What say you?" Ms. Cooper asked.

"What choice do I have? This is the only way I'm gonna get FUC'd," she growled, eyes flashing at Dario.

Chickee was this close to her dream job. She just had to get in bed with the enemy.

Er.

Metaphorically speaking.

Cluck cluck.

3

—————

"I can't believe you agreed to this," Dario Marten said, shocked to his core the little female had said yes.

Sure, he wanted to be back out in the field, but like this? With her? No. It was impossible.

"Are we flying coach?" Chickee asked, ignoring his little panic attack.

Dario didn't know if he should be grateful or annoyed. How could she be so calm? His palms were sweating, and he didn't know whether to shake her or kiss her. For fuck's sake, when had she grown up? The Chickee of his TV memories was a skinny little thing who always seemed to trip over her own feet and make the audience laugh at every turn.

God, she was funny. But she was smart, too, not that the cameras followed much of that aspect of her life. He'd noticed the good grades she'd always seemed proud of. Papers with bright, shining A's her mother would ignore. Genevieve Prinz was quite a piece of work, immature and fake. Dario had never liked her.

She would always dismiss Chickee and tell her to model whatever new clothes or gadgets sponsors had sent for her to try out. It was the reality TV equivalent of running ads. He understood all too well how quick the money came and went for people like that. Chickee was nothing but a cash cow for Genevieve Prinz. A veritable golden goose, *er*, chicken.

She's grown up good, he mused, checking her out beneath his thick lashes. She wore a pair of jeans outlining her sumptuous curves, curves she had not had as a child star. She'd matured beautifully, and in all the right places. Even tried to hide her magnificent breasts from his gaze with a bulky sweatshirt, but Christ, talk about mission impossible.

Dario did not mean to sound like a pig. He simply loved the female form. It was true he adored women all over the world, but no one held his interest just lately. No one until he'd run into a certain hen with a heavenly body. Even his tayra took note.

Grrrr.

"Coach? I never fly coach. No, these are first class," he grumbled, looking at the ticket in his hand.

"First class? Nice," she murmured, pulling on the one piece of luggage she'd brought.

Dario frowned.

"How did you pack an evening gown in there? You will have to wear one, you know." He stated the obvious.

"Yes. I know how award ceremonies work, and to answer your question, I didn't," she replied.

Chickee's cheeks brightened, and he scented her embarrassment but had no idea why she responded that way to his question. It was innocent enough.

"Look, it's been a few years for me since I was in the spotlight, and well, I gained a few pounds, Mr. Marten. Don't worry. I have an appointment at a boutique in town," she mumbled.

"You mean since you were a child? Of course you did. You look great. And call me Dario," he said, a low growl climbing its way out of his throat.

Grrrr.

He could hardly have stopped it. His inner beastie had been poking his head up to better see and smell the tiny beauty since they'd gotten in the car together that morning to head for the airport. The hardy little hen was cute as a button in her yellow capri pants and white sweater. She looked fresh as a daisy and smelled as sweet. Like peach-flavored wine and just as heady.

"Dario?"

"Yes, we are supposed to be dating. Dario seems more appropriate. But if you have a kink and want to call me Mr. Marten in bed, just tell me, sweetheart, and I'll try to get on board with that," he whispered in her ear, noting the little shiver that danced its way up her spine.

Hot little hen. And the more time he spent with her, the hotter she appeared to Dario. His tayra growled, the mustelid more than interested in the fair-haired fowl.

"You wish," she replied, her voice a touch trembly.

He hoped like hell her sexy little reaction was because of him. Knowing his closeness affected a woman did something to a man. Dario could not deny he found the sweet blonde chick hella good-looking.

Curves for miles, pretty pink lips, and an adorable, care-free air that seemed to be a natural part of her person, Chickee was simply stunning. He placed a hand on her lower back, guiding her in front of him as they passed through TSA to board the plane. Playing the possessive paramour seemed to come naturally, though Dario was not into being the other man.

"You are not leaving a boyfriend or lover home alone

while we work, are you?" he whispered and noted her eyebrows shooting straight into her hairline.

"What? No! I mean you are my only, *um*, lover," she replied, looking around pointedly at the other passengers.

"No worries, sweetheart. We are surrounded by humans. No one can hear me but you when I talk this low," he said, a curl of a smile teasing at the corner of his mouth.

Dario grinned, noting her squeak when his hand dipped slightly to caress the curve of her perfectly plump bottom. If he was not careful, this little ruse was going to go straight to his head. But if they were going to sell it, he had to get her used to him.

"What are you doing?" she hissed as they waited for the gate agent to finish the welcome speech before calling for first-class passengers to board.

"Nothing I would not do to any woman I was dating, sweetheart," he murmured, taking a moment to catch her earlobe between his teeth.

Tayras loved to nibble.

"We are not really dating," she whispered back, her small hands on his chest.

Dario really liked the way they felt there. The sexy, sweet female was damn cute without even realizing it. And didn't that make her even more attractive? He dipped his head again, nuzzling her neck and breathing in her scent.

Grrrr.

"You're right. We should announce our engagement," he replied, finding himself addicted to the easy way she blushed at his words.

"I'm not kidding, Dario. Fake, remember?"

"Neither am I, Chickee my sweet. Come on. They are calling our seats," he said, guiding her to their assigned row.

Unfortunately, first class did not mean they were alone.

Dario was hoping to spend the next few hours teasing smiles and blushes from the surprisingly shy hen shifter, but almost as soon as they sat down, another couple took the row beside them.

The man looked familiar with an orangey fake-tan glow to his skin and a ridiculous amount of chest hair on display. He had gold rings on all of his fingers and dark glasses covering most of his face. The woman with him was a bottle blonde, not at all like his Chickee's own naturally pale locks, and her fake tan was only outdone by her boob implants and the cosmetic surgery so obvious on her face.

"Hey, aren't you that kid from *Hatched*? OMG! Milo, look. It's Chickee from *Hatched*! I used to watch your show aaaaal-llll the time," screeched the female.

"Thank you," Chickee replied magnanimously.

Her smile seemed authentic, but Dario could tell from the tightness of her eyes and the subtle increase to her heartbeat that she was uncomfortable. He took her hand in his and squeezed.

"OMG! You have been out of the spotlight for years! I bet that hurt, huh? So why you goin' to the CANS? Got any prospects for a *Hatched 2*? My guy here is a big producer. Maybe he can help you out with that," she said, elbowing the large, mostly orange man.

"Oh, uh. That's not necessary," Chickee began.

Dario felt her rising panic, and it made his tayra growl. The stranger did not mean to upset Chickee, but still... Fake girlfriend or not, Dario could not allow this to continue.

"Actually, we are just on a personal trip," he said with a stiff smile, leaning back when the woman set her predatory eyes on him.

"Oh, you are a looker and protective too," the stranger replied and snorted unattractively.

"Um, thanks anyway," Chickee cut her off. "I'm not looking to renew anything. We are just going to town for a quiet getaway."

"Oh, I see."

"Sweetheart, stop yapping and let those people be. I gotta get some shuteye before I meet with Marten," her companion grumbled, turning slightly and dismissing Chickee and Dario both.

Thank fuck.

Dario frowned. He hadn't missed the name the man had dropped. This man was meeting his father. He sniffed.

Shifter?

No.

He smelled human. And gross. Like BO and tanning oil.

Eww.

"Did you hear that?" Chickee whispered in his ear.

Fuck yes. Her warm breath tickled his skin, and when he gazed into her big green eyes, it was easy to get lost in them. He held himself still, refusing to give in to the temptation to shiver.

Pretty little chick.

Mine.

What?

No.

Yep.

Want.

"I heard him. I'm on it. Better get some rest, cutie," Dario replied, dropping a kiss on her little button nose.

Her eyes widened in question, and he tilted his head slightly. The nosy female beside them was still watching. Good thing her dull human senses would never pick up on what they were saying, and without that, it just looked like they were whispering, like lovers were wont to do.

"If you kiss me again without asking, I'll peck your eyes out, honey," she cooed, and Dario chuckled softly.

"Next time, you'll ask for it, sweet chick," he replied with a wink.

Cocky was his usual MO, but it was not like he had no reason to be. The Marten men were known gigolos. His ancestor had provided the inspiration for the actual *Don Juan* stories.

Having hailed from Spain, Dario's great-great-great-grandfather, *Juan Marteno*, settled in South America in his efforts to outrun the angry husbands and spouses of several women he had, *er*, relationships with back in Seville. Indeed, Dario's lineage was full of lotharios and libertines, even if he chose a more sedate route himself.

Of course, now that he was thrown into a fake relationship with the charming chickadee, Dario had to admit he kind of liked it. She snoozed beside him. Her face looked so very pretty in its relaxed pose. Her blonde hair smelled good, like peach blossoms and spring rain.

Dario liked the way her eyebrows and lashes were darker, brushing against her pale skin just right. She really was so very pretty. He likened her face to an artist's sketch he'd seen and wondered if the Fates themselves had taken the time to choose the palette of colors that made up her beautiful visage.

The rest of the flight was uneventful. Dario stayed awake and alert, determined to make sure Chickee's sleep went undisturbed. Why he should feel so protective of her he did not know, but all it took was one click from the woman's camera phone in front of them for him to lose his cool.

"What was that?" Chickee asked, snapping awake as if she knew her privacy had just been violated.

Probably did. Poor thing.

"It's nothing, sweetheart. Get some rest," he whispered.

When she did fall back asleep, his chest swelled with pride. Whether she admitted it or not, some part of her felt safe enough with him to sleep. Dario tapped on the chair in front of him and was met with the garishly made-up face of the stranger who'd brazenly stolen a moment of Chickee's rest.

"Hey, can I see your phone?"

"Excuse me? Why would you want to do that?"

"Well, you took a picture of my fiancée, and I wanted to make sure you got the best light," he said, smiling charmingly at the female.

"You mean, you aren't angry?" she asked cautiously.

"Angry? Why would I be angry? She is famous, after all," he replied, hand outstretched.

The woman returned his smile, handing over the phone, and Dario continued to charm her while he scrolled through her pictures, sending a horrifying pic she'd snapped of herself before and after surgery to his phone.

"What are you doing?" she asked, reaching for the device, but Dario simply leaned back and held it aloft while he scrolled and sent himself snap after snap of the woman along with some texts he was certain she would rather were kept private.

"Well, Ms. Simpson, what I am doing is making myself a nice little file in case you decide to invade my fiancée's privacy again. I will make sure these find their way to every social media and news outlet available."

"You deleted the pic I took. How dare you!" she whisper-screamed.

"How dare I? You are the one trespassing here. Go on, try to take another picture, and I assure you I will find out. If you do, then these will find themselves blasted over every social media outlet out there, Ms. Simpson. Yes, I know who you are, and I know who your husband is," Dario threatened, holding his phone to reveal the images he'd sent himself from her phone.

"Some of these are very interesting, Ms. Simpson."

"So what? Everyone in Hollywood gets plastic surgery. Those before and after pics are old news," she said haughtily.

"True, but I am not talking about the images of your plastic surgeries, rather the ones hidden inside those files. I assume your husband does not know about the company you keep when he is out of town?" Dario asked.

"Those files are secret," she hissed.

"Nothing is secret if you keep a record, ma'am. I suggest deleting them."

"You are no gentleman!"

"Nope. I'm a weasel," he replied with a snarled grin.

"Tayra," Chickee corrected him, and he turned his head, startled.

Dario's heart pounded as he stared into her big green eyes. How long had the little chick been awake? She blinked slowly, and Dario felt the chink in his armor grow. He knew better than to get attached to anyone.

Tayras were not meant to be part of a pairing, and yet, when she looked at him like that, with admiration and gratitude shining in her emerald depths, Dario could not help but hope. Maybe his father was wrong about his kind. Maybe he could find happiness with one person. Even if she was his sworn enemy.

"Thank you," she whispered, ignoring the woman in front of them as she harrumphed and turned in her seat.

"My pleasure," he returned and was shocked that he meant it.

With any luck, this mission might wind up very pleasurable indeed for the two of them. The signal to fasten their seatbelts flashed, and Dario checked Chickee's before his, noting her nervousness as the plane hit some turbulence.

"You can hold my hand if you're nervous, sweetheart."

She was biting her lower lip, a habit she had since she was a child, and Dario felt an overwhelming urge to ease her tension. Her hand slipped over his, and he caught it, squeezing her fingers gently until they passed through the bumpy patches of air that had them jostling in their seats.

The pilot's voice filtered through the cabin. *"Sorry about that, ladies and gentlemen, the weather is clearing and we will arrive at JFK in about three hours. We hope you enjoy the rest of the flight."*

Chickee cleared her throat and stood up once the fasten-seat-belt sign turned off, excusing herself for the restroom. It was Dario's turn to chew his lip. The other passengers were asleep, and the nasty woman in front of them had headphones on and was snickering over whatever hellish movie she was watching. Good for her.

Dario's mind was otherwise occupied. His brain filled with images of what he recalled from Chickee's past. He'd been a kid, a few years younger than the reality star, and by the time he was old enough to follow the frenzy that revolved around *Hatched*, he'd already become disillusioned with the father he had once idolized.

Chickee really had it rough, growing up under a veritable avalanche of flashing lights and seedy headlines. Her adoptive mother was a piece of work, selling her daughter's privacy for money. And fuck Dario's father for being part of the problem.

"Are you okay?" she asked softly, having returned from the restroom.

Crap. He didn't even realize he'd been growling, but the animal inside him was pissed off. He did not like to think of her upset or having to deal with all of that. Dario had not considered how volatile a situation this was for her.

"Are *you* okay? Going back to the spotlight, I mean?" he asked, low enough that the humans wouldn't hear.

"Well, it's not my ideal situation, but I've been wanting the opportunity to be an agent," she replied honestly.

"Are you sure?"

"I can handle it," she said, but her voice wavered at the end.

Dario nodded. He would not question her resolve. She did not deserve that and, especially, not from him. But for the first time in his life, Dario had a mission completely different from what his bosses had assigned him.

His tayra finally had a purpose—keeping Chickee safe.

4

"This is not the hotel," Dario observed.

"Thank you, Captain Obvious," she muttered.

He leaned over her in the cab to better view the street where she'd asked the cabbie to pull over. The fact he'd brushed against her boobs with his arm was probably a coincidence; the things were rather huge and in the way. Nevertheless, a shiver of awareness raced through her at the unintentional touch.

"Pardon me," he said, smirking, and Chickee knew he'd done it on purpose. "You know, if you're feeling down, I can feel you up," he said, waggling his eyebrows and making a dorky face.

"Ugh, you are such a weasel," she muttered, trying hard not to laugh.

Chickee pushed the sly mustelid off her, not caring that she bopped his nose with her purse in the process. Served him right, getting fresh with her.

"Ouch!"

"Don't be such a crybaby," she muttered.

"No, you're right. My bad. Just trying to make you smile,

sweetheart," Dario said, sounding silly since he was pinching his nose to ease the pain.

Bok bok.

Served him right. But Chickee had no time to spare thinking about a Marten's pain. She was about to go into the lion's den.

"Seriously, Chickee, what's wrong?" he asked, suddenly very close to her.

"It's been a while since I did this kind of shopping. I've changed a lot since then," she confessed.

"Change is good, Chickee Prinz. I feel bad for the people stuck. And in case you're worried about your appearance and how people will react to you, know this. I think you are a knockout."

"You do?"

"I do. In case you don't believe me," he whispered and pulled her against him, allowing her to feel the rock-hard evidence of his attraction.

Chickie gulped, and Dario growled, settling his lips over hers in a smooth, three-second-long kiss that left her panting for more.

"Go get something befitting the gorgeous little badass you are, sweetheart. I'll be waiting for you right here," he told her with one of his wicked, panty-melting grins.

Fucking Marten male. They were all like this. Chickee should not be so easily fooled, and yet, there was something about Dario that made her heart stutter in her chest and her inner hen cluck like crazy.

"I'll be back in a few."

Chickee gave him a small wave and turned around. Waving? Really? What was wrong with her?

Bok bok.

Fidgeting with her purse as she stepped into the small

boutique on West 37th Street, Chickee's nerves threatened to get the best of her. She hated shopping. Especially when people recognized her and compared her present self to her old self.

Sad bok.

The proprietor, Amelia, was the sole designer and seamstress for Skin Deep. Her mission was to provide couture gowns for curvy women—the kind Chickee's old life deemed unworthy of attention.

"Should I hold the cab?" Dario asked, his dark eyes questioning.

"Please do. I will be fifteen minutes," she told him quietly.

They'd reached some sort of odd truce on the airplane, and Chickee was not sure just how she felt about the man. Dario had been reserved and silent for most of the ride through Manhattan. No, she had not disclosed her plan to do a little shopping first, but so what? Anyway, she still did not trust him.

How could she? He was the son of the most notorious media mogul in the world. A real weasel of a man. What would Gabriel Marten say if he saw his son escorting the *starlet who got away* all over town like some towering, ridiculously good-looking bodyguard? He would want Dario to give him the inside scoop.

Whatever tentative truce they'd called to pull off this fake relationship, Chickee had to remember it was all for show. She could not afford to reveal intimacies about herself to Dario. He was still the enemy.

Cluck cluck.

Fine, she admitted. *He's an enemy with impeccable manners.* He'd been holding doors open for her and making sure she was comfortable every inch of this trip.

And, yes, he'd even stuck up for her on the plane when that horrible woman had snapped pictures of her sleeping.

But Chickee still had secrets and insecurities. As a reality star, she'd spent years fighting eating disorders to stay slim for the cameras and fans of *Hatched*. Her departure from the spotlight meant she could finally live her life the way she wanted to, and, yes, that meant eating carbs.

Chickee no longer tortured or starved herself to fit into the mold people like Gabriel Marten and her mother had made for her. She was very aware of her curvier-than-average size, and honestly, after finding out she was a shifter, it all made sense.

Her big boobs and plump thighs were pretty common among chickens, especially Jersey Giants. She would not apologize for them any longer. For couture befitting ladies who looked like Chickee, Skin Deep was the very best.

That did not mean she wanted to prance around in all her chubby glory in front of Dario. The tall, sexy tayra had his pick of gorgeous women. She'd been hyperaware of every move the man made since running into him at FUCN'A. Not that she would admit it.

Fine, she was chicken. Literally and figuratively.

The fact he flustered her at all was embarrassing as heck. Chickee was simply unused to the attention. Trust was hard for her. And trusting a Marten? Impossible.

It's just for a few days, she thought, bolstering her resolve. A few days of intense dark stares, slightly accented whispers, and perhaps more of that hand-holding she'd enjoyed so much on the plane.

Yes, please.

"Welcome! Ms. Prince, I'm Amelia. I have an assortment of gowns for you back here. I know we will find something

you'll love," the friendly woman said with a big smile on her
lips.

Chickee sure hoped so. If she was getting back in the
spotlight, she needed to look good. And, no, it had nothing
at all to do with the sexy shifter waiting outside.

Liar.

"That was more than fifteen minutes," Dario said as
Chickee walked outside, loaded down with bags.

His grin told her he was not really mad, and when he
took her things and placed them in the trunk, well, she
almost swooned. Manners were a hot commodity for
Chickee since so few people seemed to have them.

"Sorry," she muttered.

"Don't be. If there is one thing a man should always be
patient with, it's his woman."

"Don't you mean *a* woman?"

"Perhaps," he replied, dark eyes shining with mirth.

He gave the driver directions to the hotel, and Chickee
sat back and enjoyed the sights as they inched their way
through traffic. The city was abuzz with excitement. She'd
spent a few months here in her teenaged years and was
surprised to find she had missed the East Coast.

"Are you hungry?" Dario asked.

Chickee frowned, wondering if that was a jibe. But that
only lasted a moment since she could hear his own stomach
growling. Grinning, she nodded and told the cab to pull
over at the next corner near a sidewalk vendor. Three pret-
zels, six knishes, and two falafel sandwiches later, they
made their way to the hotel amid a whirlwind of flashing
lights and microphones thrust in her face.

"Crap. This is a shitshow," Dario growled as he considered their next move.

"It can't be helped," she said, biting her lip nervously.

"Are you sure you want to do this?"

"To protect the shifter secret?" she whispered so only he could hear, nodding her head.

"Brave girl," he replied, taking her hand as he pulled her out of the vehicle.

Dario barked instructions at the bellhop, who loaded their belongings onto a cart. The dozen reporters and photographers were trying to get closer, asking impossibly invasive questions as they tried to corner her. Chickee ducked her head, thankful for the large sunglasses Dario had slipped on her face before they exited the vehicle.

"Give us room, please," he told the reporters, expertly using his body as a shield to block her from the unwanted attention.

"Chickee, what have you been doing on hiatus from the show?"

"Is it true *Hatched 2* is in the works?"

"Are you still estranged from your mother?"

"Who's the stud, Chickee?"

"Can you tell us when you let yourself go?"

"The fuck did you say?" Dario snarled, and Chickee grabbed his arm, pulling him back to her.

"Let it go," she hissed. "I need you with me."

Dario shoved the asshole back a few paces then tucked Chickee under his arm. She heard the telltale click of the cameras though. The paparazzi was going to have a field day with images of Dario shoving that photographer away from her.

Chickee hated this part. Always had. The walk to the front door seemed to take forever. But for one glorious moment, Dario Marten had stood there and blocked her from everything that was going on. He'd offered her the protection of his body, and greedy little chicken that she was, she took it.

Whispers reached her ears as the soulless reporters outside figured out who Dario was, and she bit her lip, waiting for the moment he regretted giving them what they came for. Only—it didn't happen. Dario led her through the busy lobby, signaling the manager with a nod as he brought her to the service elevators in the back.

"How did you know where these elevators were?" she asked dumbly.

"While you slept on the plane, I researched the hotel and venue for the awards tomorrow night. We are already checked in and the bags will be brought up. I do not want you to worry about your safety while we are here, Chickee. I got you," he told her.

And he did. Christ, help her.

Dangerous, sexy, cunning tayra.

5

Upstairs in their one bedroom, Chickee exhaled the breath she'd been holding. Holy crap. She was going to be stuck in there. With him. All. Night. Long.

"Okay, uh, we should go over how we are going to behave in public," she began, earning her a quick glance from the tall, handsome male.

"What do you mean? I thought we handled that fine."

"Yes, I mean you were a little, um, forceful with that photographer. No need to go over the top like that with this little performance of ours," she replied, secretly thrilled he'd gone to bat for her. No one ever had before. Even if it was fake.

Cluck.

"I am afraid that was not put on, Chickee. I do not like when people are disrespectful of women in general, and with you, I like it even less."

Truth.

One thing being a shifter had taught her was how to tell when someone was lying. Dario displayed none of the telltale signs of fibbing or lying or any such thing. He honestly did not like when she was disrespected.

Bok bok.

Well, throw her for a loop. Why doesn't he? The man was making her question everything she knew about the Marten men. He was just as good-looking as the rest of them, even more so. But where she'd expected a cocky boy who flirted outrageously and used women like tissues, she found a thoughtful man with an irresistible protective streak.

"Why?"

"Because, Chickee, you deserve better than that," Dario replied. "You have a hair," he murmured, brushing his fingertips across her cheek to move the errant strand.

Dario made a clicking sound with his tongue. He sucked in a sharp breath as if he, too, felt the electrical current zipping through her entire body from the gentle brush of his fingers on her face. His hand hovered there a moment too long to be accidental, and Chickee stopped breathing. Was it possible the tantalizing tayra was taken with her too?

Bok bok?

Her inner hen was clucking madly with curiosity. Was Dario as devious as his weaselly relatives? Or was there more than met the eye when it came to this mustelid? She just was not sure.

Hmm. Bok. Bok. BOK!

"Are you okay?" he asked, staring at her with intensity swirling in his molten gaze.

She loved the color of his eyes. Like rich coffee, the brown coloring was so dark and deep she could feel the burn before she sipped, but it was always worth it. But were a few minutes of physical pleasure with Dario worth the risk to her heart?

Chickee frowned hard. These kinds of thoughts could not be good for her personal growth and development. It was difficult enough learning to love herself after her turbulent childhood, but trusting others was her ultimate downfall. Especially with the opposite sex.

Good-looking men who happened to cross her path often turned out to be users and losers. Disappointment followed each relationship she had ever tried to have, and she was so not in the market for another broken heart. No matter how sexy Dario's grin was or how good he smelled —*and yes, the man smelled amazing, even better than buttered popcorn*—Chickee was better off leaving well enough alone.

She did not need to add to the sorry, albeit short, list of fuckups she'd unfortunately dated. But there was just something about the tayra that was driving her bonkers. He was just sooooo cute. And sweet. Definitely sweet.

Cluckity cluck cluck.

Her impromptu crush could not have come at a worse time. FUC finally wanted her for a job, and she needed to remain professional. That meant ignoring her screaming girly bits.

What if we just peck him on the mouth once? Or twice?

Yeah. Twice was good.

No! Stop it.

Sad cluck.

Dammit. Was it getting warm in here? She felt flustered and achy, and dammit, he was going to smell her need if she did not do something about it.

Change the subject. Good clucking idea!

Chickee sucked in a breath and walked backward a few steps, adding some much-needed space between them.

"So, did we get any updates from FUC?" she asked, a little too brightly.

"Let me check," Dario replied, pulling his cell phone from his pocket. "Ah. Seems my handler, Chase Brown-smith, has some info for us about a PRIC who is looking for info."

"A prick?" Confusion marred her face for a moment before she remembered what they were talking about. "Oh! You mean a PRIC! A *Private Resourceful Investigative Consultant*, right? Who?"

"Not sure," he muttered.

A beep sounded from both Chickee's and Dario's phones. She opened her message first, but Dario was the one who read it aloud.

"The CANS take place tomorrow, and there is a rehearsal tonight, followed by a small dinner afterward for the announcers and their plus-ones. That means us. We have to be in the lobby in two hours."

"Oh. Okay, well, *um*, I'll take a shower and get dressed. Unless you want to go first?" she asked, feeling nervous all of a sudden.

Dario's eyes darkened, and he shook his head, taking a step back. Sly weasel, giving her space when she needed it. Chickee was going to have to watch herself with this one. Cute sexy guys like him.

Danger. Bok bok. Danger.

"That's all right. You go first. I will be here watching the pre-award highlights for anything we can use in our investigation," he said, grabbing the remote.

"Okay," Chickee whispered.

She felt his eyes on her. But when she looked back, he was already watching the television screen, humming along with whatever song was on. He had a nice, deep voice. Pleasantly surprised when he started singing softly with the live band on TV, Chickee forced her legs to start moving.

Well, this is awkward.

Cluck cluck cluck.

She grabbed her bag of toiletries, heading for the bathroom. Holy crap. Heart pounding, breath barely making its way in and out of her lungs, she turned on the shower, hoping to drown out the sounds of her panic. What was wrong with her? This was not a romantic getaway. They were not really dating.

But we could be.

No.

Cluck.

Damn stubborn hen. Chickee growled. Dario Marten was not interested in her. Not now. Not ever. Best she recognized that before she allowed her overactive imagination to run away with her. Something the little chickadee could not afford to do. She was here on her first FUC assignment, not to go gaga over some untrustworthy weasel.

Tayra, her inner chick corrected.

Fine. She could acknowledge the difference. Dario was a tayra, not a weasel. A sexy, studly tayra shifter with no mate as far as she knew—and, yes, she'd already checked. He also had a set of washboard abs she was sure she could bounce a coin off of, a pair of killer soccer-player thighs, two big, long-fingered hands, and a couple of dreamy bedroom eyes she could get lost in.

Dario Marten had hit the genetic jackpot. Unlike Chickee, who'd had to starve herself when she was a young, unwilling starlet, he was the epitome of shifter good looks. And if she were smart, Chickee would reap the rewards.

But who was she kidding? She had a handful of years on him, as he was so kind to point out—*jerk*—not to mention a couple of pounds. That whole thing about chicken legs being skinny was a total lie. Chickee had thunder thighs, oversized breasts, which she considered having reduced several times, and naturally cushy buttocks.

My butt is cute, cluck you very much.

Why all this self-hate? She'd spent years tying herself in metaphorical knots to fit what society thought she should be. Countless hours with wardrobe and makeup consultants. She'd never even picked out her own hairstyle until she was sixteen years old.

"Mom, can I cut my hair like this?"

Thirteen-year-old Chickee lifted the clip she'd gotten from the town newspaper showcasing a young girl from a local soccer team with chin-length hair. Chickee thought it looked cute and fresh and wanted to try it, but she knew the drill. Any changes to her appearance had to be approved first.

"What? Oh, no, no short hair," her adoptive mother said, looking up from her place on the massage bed.

Heidi, her German masseuse, stopped working as Genevieve Prinz sat up to glare at her daughter.

"But why? I mean I thought they were going to let me try out for soccer this year, and this is how everyone has their hair for the town team."

"Chickee, I said I would ask, and that is all I can do. You won't have time to be on any team. The schedule for this season is going to be twice as long as last season. That means more camera time, Chickadee. The ratings are way up, and the fans want to see everything, especially since you are going to high school next year."

"Is that all you care about?"

"Now, don't get all morose, Chickee. This is important. You love Hatched!*"*

"I think you mean you *love* Hatched, *Mom."*

"Oh, come on. Where would you be without this show? Without me? When I found you in that orphanage, you were just

this helpless, scrawny thing. I lost my husband too soon to cancer, and I needed something to love."

"Do you though, Mom?"

"Do I what?"

"Love me."

"Don't be ridiculous, Chickee," Mom said dismissively. "Now, the producers already emailed with the expectations for your looks. Long hair is in. So..." Mom told her, a large grin on her heavily made-up face.

"So, what? My hair is already long," Chickee said, dread filling her.

"We're going to make it even longer with some added dark brown extensions to really highlight your eyes. The director says we need to draw attention away from your boobs. I mean, really, Chickee, you have to stop the snacking between meals! And for the love of God, no more popcorn and absolutely no chocolate."

That was just one in a long line of miserable memories from her own personal mommy dearest. She hadn't spoken to Genevieve Prinz in years. Not since she'd found Chickee shifted in her bathroom, just another fowl running afoul. By then, she was so dependent on the money Chickee brought home, Genevieve was willing to do anything to hide her adopted daughter's freakish tendencies. Including lie.

The couple of years after were some of the worst of Chickee's life. Her shifts were unpredictable and painful. After all, it was not easy to go from a buck-fifty teenager to ten pounds of hen. Hell, even hitting a hundred and fifty pounds had become more and more difficult for her. She was starving herself, angry at the world, and she didn't know shit about cluck when it came to her animal.

Cluckity cluck.

Lucky was the day she ran into her first FUC agent. After that, Chickee learned what she was—a chicken without a flock. But at least Chickee knew her obsession for popcorn was part of her supernatural makeup and not just a chubby-girl thing.

"Chicken shifters are rare, but they do exist, typically in small flocks. We have not been able to locate yours, Ms. Prinz," Viktor had said. *"But you have a place here, if you want it."*

For the first time since she'd run away from the spotlight, Chickee had found a home. And here she was, risking her sense of self-worth to pay back the FUCs who'd given her peace of mind. She could do this. After all, she wasn't chicken.

Cluck cluck.

If working with Dario Marten was the price she had to pay for fulfilling her dreams and repaying her debts, Chickee would just have to grin and bear it. She could get through a few days of soulless photographers and reporters breathing down her neck, and she could do it while pretending to be Dario's girlfriend, *er*, fiancée.

Easy peasy.

She just had to remember to take it slow, ignore the tempting tayra's sex appeal, and keep hold of her heart while she was at it. He was a born ladies' man. He probably did not even realize the effect his smiles had on unsuspecting women. *Scratch that.*

The man was a Marten. He definitely knew he left a trail of wet panties whenever he walked into a room. It was ridiculous how attractive he was. But Chickee was only human, sorta. And she could not deny she was just another thunderstruck female at the mercy of Dario Marten's all-powerful charisma.

That little touch he'd given her...pure chemistry. But that was all it was. A chemical reaction to certain stimuli. There was nothing special about his touches.

Bok bok.

Chickee shivered, ignoring her snarky hen as she stripped out of her traveling clothes. She paused as Dario's rich baritone floated through the door. Holy. Crap. The man sang too? Like really sang. He was belting like Marc Anthony, and her girly bits were throbbing like a swarm of screaming groupies at a concert.

Was there anything sexier than a man with a voice that gave her chills? Um. Yeah. How about a man with a six-pack and eyes like dark chocolate?

Cluck. Cluck. CLUCK.

All she could do was stand there and listen while naked. Wait. She was naked. And he was right there. Well, not *there* there but close enough. Her heart started thudding loudly in her chest.

Bumbum bumbum bumbum.

Would he hear if she reached between her legs to ease the ache he'd conjured with hardly any effort at all? Should she risk it? His spicy male scent wafted through the small space between the door and the tiled floor of the hotel bathroom, and she inhaled.

A desperate-sounding mewl escaped her lips. There was only so much teasing a girl could take. She turned the handle, filling the bathroom with steam and wishing like hell the noise from the shower would drown out his seductive voice. It didn't, of course.

Curse you, shifter hearing!

Maybe if she could just stop picturing Dario naked, she could get on with her shower, get dressed, and prepare for the role she had to play.

You mean his girlfriend, right? You're supposed to be his girl, Chickee. So, sexy fun times are technically okay then. Right?

She was sick. That was the only way to justify the turn of

her thoughts. Sick and sex-starved and way too close to the mouthwatering mustelid. But man oh man, the guy was as fine as any FUC she'd ever seen, and Chickee had seen a ton of agents.

Not just as a guest professor, teaching the art of makeup and disguise, but back when she was a newly moved to Canada ex-pat, looking for her shifter roots. Viktor Smith had introduced her to a whole slew of good-looking agents. Still, she was hard-pressed to find one as handsome as the tayra in the next room.

What? No. The man is the enemy, she reminded herself.

How annoying to find Chickee's inner hen was having none of her badmouthing Dario! When had he become hers to defend? Seriously, she'd really like to know. The man's father was responsible for some of the worst incidents in her life. But Dario wasn't. In fact, he had been nothing but protective and kind since they'd left the Academy.

Ignoring the surprisingly on-key rendition of Dario's next song, "Livin' La Vida Loca," was proving impossible. She snorted. The man was ridiculous. And yet, he made Chickee laugh. Really laugh. Plus, she'd napped beside him on the plane. When had she ever felt comfortable enough around a man to doze off? Wasn't that interesting and refreshing?

Better get your head on straight, chicken.

She could not afford to mess this opportunity up because of her stupid hormones. It had been quite a while since she'd enjoyed any between-the-sheets time with a real live man. And these sheets were probably 2000-count, Egyptian cotton.

Okay, reasons we should not consider banging the weasel:

A) He's your enemy. But not really.

> *His father is your enemy. And Dario doesn't talk to his father anymore.*

> *Shit. There goes A.*

B) He's younger than you.

> *So? Age is just a number. Plenty of women go with younger men.*

C) You've added about forty pounds to your person since the last Hatched *episode aired.*

> *And? I'm naturally curvy. I am also a full-grown woman, not a teenager exploited by her mother and the media. Besides, he did not seem to mind the extra poundage when he was holding my hand and whispering in my ear on the plane.*

D) Um. Crap. What was D again?

> *Face it, Chickee. You want him.*

> *Go cluck yourself.*

She heaved a sigh, totally frustrated with her inner voice.

"Chickee? Are you all right?" Dario called through the door.

"Bok!" she screeched, jumping at the interruption.

Of course, that triggered a random set of unfortunate events to occur. She got shampoo in her eye, banged her elbow on the shower handle, and slipped and fell on her rear while managing not to hear the click of the door opening.

"Chickee! Are you okay?" he asked, opening the curtain.

Pause.

"What are you doing?" Dario asked, his voice sounding slightly amused and a little bit husky.

She was blinded by the soap. Her butt hurt from the fall. She was horny as fuck. And to top it all off, Dario had just barged in to see her butt-ass naked with suds in her face? This was too much. Chickee did the only thing she could do.

She cluck-screamed.

"Bok BOKKKKK!"

6

Dario tried everything he could think of to stop imagining Chickee, the foxy little fowl, naked and wet from the shower and separated from him by a measly hollow-core door. Okay. That was *so* not helping.

He was completely flummoxed by his increasing attraction to the headstrong hen. He was a knight-in-shining-designer-suit kinda guy, but she was no damsel in distress. Chickee did not need to be rescued. She was tough as nails, a product of an upbringing he would not wish on anyone, and Dario knew just how much it had affected her.

She might cluck and snarl about it, but he saw the truth. Hell, he'd had a front-row seat to it. Growing up a Marten meant learning the family business from the time he could read and write, which was a precocious two-and-three-quarters years old for the son of the most hated mustelid on the planet. He'd started earlier than any of his siblings. *Take that, losers!*

Fine, he was still very competitive with his brothers. But sibling rivalry was healthy, right? At any rate, it taught him survival skills that rivaled the most highly trained FUCs Dario had ever come across.

But what was he doing, salivating over the one female in the universe who had every cause to hate him? *The World According to Marten* was a scandalous tabloid that had somehow survived for six generations in the human world, jumping mediums from paper to screen without faltering. But that was not all.

Apparently, his father had also become a producer of reality television, hiding that little factoid from Dario. To think his own dad was responsible for *Hatched* made his skin crawl. Sure, people loved the series, and the reruns still streamed on certain paid subscription services, but Chickee had been hurt. And that was seriously not okay.

Grrrr.

The sound of her pained chirp, followed by a fall and a muffled screech, had Dario rushing across the room. He should respect her privacy, but she could be hurt, bleeding even. He couldn't do nothing. With a little force, he broke the lock on the door and tore the curtain back.

"Chickee! Are you okay?"

Dario paused as he took her in. No blood. Good. She appeared whole and unharmed. And, oh, fuck yes, she was naked.

"What are you doing?" Dario asked, his voice sounding slightly amused.

Dario bit back the grin that threatened to crack his face. Gorgeous little hen was gloriously naked, her luscious bottom on the floor of the tiled shower, eyes closed while soap suds threatened to fill them, rubbing her red elbow.

Holy hell, she was cute.

"One minute, sweetheart," he murmured, grabbing a washcloth and wetting it before handing it to her.

"Owie, owie, owieeee! It burns," she wailed.

"Shhh. I'm here. It's going to be okay. Now, tilt your head back," he growled, climbing into the shower with her and tilting her head beneath the spray of cooling water.

He turned the handle to make the water cool in order to wash the soap from her face, uncaring that he was still wearing his slacks and shirt. At least he'd taken off his shoes earlier. Hell, he'd done that and more to distract him from his growing attraction to his temporary FUC partner.

Gulp.

Dario had tried to stay away. He'd flipped through the channels, unpacked both their belongings, and tried like hell to not think about the naked woman in the shower.

Chickee surprised him in ways he had not expected. And the hits just kept on coming. She was not the spoiled brat he'd taken for granted that a former child star would be. Truthfully, he knew a little about her past and was peripherally aware of the role Marten Press had played in the events that had shaped and ultimately hurt this woman's life. Even then, she was remarkably resilient. She did not walk around complaining about the hand she'd been dealt. Rather, she set about making changes. Got emancipated. Moved to Canada. Started a career teaching at FUCN'A.

To find her at the Academy, working hard for what amounted to a pittance compared to what she used to earn with her show, and with real dedication, was a total shocker. Everything he discovered made him like her even more. Despite the ghosts of her past, she was willing to brave the media for a shot at protecting all shifters. Hell, she was risking her well-earned peace and putting herself directly in the line of fire to help save them all. If he couldn't recognize that as brave, then Dario really was a weasel.

I see you, though. Courageous little hen. Not chicken at all.

"Shit. It burns," she growled.

"Blink slowly," he whispered, liking the feel of her silky skin beneath his fingers. He worked quickly, washing the soap away gently, running the cool water over her face until she breathed easier. Once she did, he realized he felt better, too.

"Okay, now?"

"Yeah," she replied.

Her green eyes were rimmed in red from the soap, but he thought they were simply beautiful. She smiled up at him and damn if parts of him didn't stand up to salute.

"Um, Dario?"

"Yes?"

"You're getting wet."

"True, my sweet chicken little," Dario murmured, not caring a fig for his ruined clothes. Awareness sizzled between them, and he captured her gaze, refusing to release it until she answered the question that was burning a hole in his mind.

"The real question, sweetheart, is, *are you*?"

His words hung between them like a flashing sign, but he did not wait for a response. Instead, he did something utterly rash, questionably stupid, and possibly career-ending.

Dario Marten kissed Chickee Prinz. In the shower. With all his clothes on.

Grrrr.

Passion exploded between them. Chickee moaned, granting him access to deepen their connection, and Dario took advantage. How could he not? She was delicious. Soft, warm, and wet—*so wet.*

"Wait! Wait a minute," she growled, shoving against his chest.

"What? Stop?" he asked, ignoring his stone-hard cock, knowing he would stop if she wanted him to—*even if it killed him.*

"If we do this, it's a one-off. Just to get it out of our systems, deal? I mean don't go falling in love with me, Marten. Neither of us want that," she said in a rush.

"If anyone falls for anyone, it will be you, sweetheart." He grinned, always the cocky bastard.

"We'll see about that," the cute little chicken quipped, snagging his bottom lip between her teeth and gripping the edge of his shirt.

"So, yes, then? We're doing this?"

"Do you need me to say it?"

"Yes."

"Then, yes, we are doing this, Marten. Now what's a girl gotta do to get a little attention around here?" she asked, biting her lip and offering him a wicked grin.

Charmingly enchanting little chicken.

"Ask me for it," he said.

"You always this needy?" she teased.

"Only since I met you, sweetheart," he told her truthfully.

"Fine. I'm a big girl. I can ask for what I want."

"What do you want, sweetheart?"

"I want you to make me come, Dario. Can you do that?"

"Yessssss," he hissed and slammed his mouth to hers before she could utter another word.

Blood rushed to his head, *er,* the other one, but Dario was deaf, dumb, and blind to everything and all but her. Only her. She was the singular most important thing right then.

It was touch or go who would fall on their ass a second time as Chickee helped Dario shed his clothes. Fuck. She was so sexy and smooth. Her petite stature fit perfectly against his taller frame. He liked that she was smaller in that way, the better to wrap his body around hers.

He snuck his tongue past her lips and growled loudly at the flavor he found there, sweet like peaches and strong like wine. Dario was drunk on her. He wrapped his fingers around the back of her neck, letting the water cascade over them as she rubbed her lips against his kiss, sliding her tongue in a rhythm as old as time.

It had been a long time since a woman had caught his attention, and that of his tayra, but Dario was on high alert now. Chickee Prinz had claimed 100 percent of his concentration, and that was before he'd come rushing through the bathroom door at the first sound of distress and found her naked and wet on the shower floor—his new favorite position, by the way.

Grrrr.

Finally freed from his clinging, wet slacks, Dario lifted Chickee off the floor. His hardened cock butted against her sweet crack, and he groaned aloud at how good she felt against him.

So soft. So sweet. So very sexy.

The foxy female fowl hissed as their skin sizzled against one another. She wrapped her legs around his waist, making him that much harder as he eagerly sought her slick entrance. Dario was big, but he'd worked to make sure she could take him. The fantastic female was built for him; he had no doubt.

"You sure about this?" he asked, giving her one last chance to back out.

"Are you always this coy?" she asked, pecking at his lip and rousing his inner animal.

"Not at all, sweetheart. Just wanna make sure you mean

it before I wreck you for anyone else," he replied, sliding his long, hard shaft between her folds.

"Stop teasing and fuck me already," she growled, and that was the straw that broke the tayra's back.

"Anything you want," he said, but little did the sexy chicken know he meant it.

Chickee might be using him to loosen up before facing down old demons, but Dario had long-term plans for the two of them. The second he pushed into her wet heat, he knew this chicken was the one for him.

He was a one-woman tayra, and she was that woman. He knew she would not agree easily, but that was all right. He had his ways. Tayras were members of the weasel family, after all. Chickee was a hen with no flock, but Dario would fix that.

He was just the man to build her a nest. To make her safe and warm. To keep her screaming his name.

"Dario! Dario! Darioooooo!"

Her walls squeezed, and Dario growled, working double time to bring another release from her heavenly body before he followed suit. Fuck, she was tight. Hot. Wet. And more than welcoming. The ripe globes of her ass felt so good in his hands, but it was her breasts that did him in.

Fuck, they were perfect. He'd never seen such beautiful mounds, tipped with pretty pink berries just begging for his mouth. So big. So soft. So tasty.

Bending his head, he sucked one plump nubbin into his mouth, loving the way her sheath tightened in response. Dario quickly found the right rhythm for his sweet chicken little.

Suck, squeeze, flex, and repeat.

The shower had turned lukewarm, but nothing was going to stop Dario from conquering the quivering little hen. His muscles tensed, teeth clamped over her shoulder but not breaking skin as he pumped into her slowly, rubbing her little bundle of nerves with every shallow thrust. Chickee's sharp claws clutched at his shoulders as she fell apart, and Dario finally let himself fall over the edge with her.

Fuck, she was perfect, clinging to him with the cold water baring down, body sated, glorious breasts smashed against his chest, and Dario's name still on her lips.

What had he done? The idea was to get her addicted to him, not the other way around. But it was too late for that. The heart-stealing hen had him head over heels for her!

"Oh, Dario, that was just... I mean wow," she whispered as she slid her legs to the bottom of the tub, gently pushing against him.

But Dario was stuck. He couldn't let go. Eyes blazing, he met her questioning stare and said the only thing his pea-sized brain could manage.

"Mine."

Uh-oh.

～

Meanwhile, via Zoom link from a garage in Downtown Jersey City...

"Is everything in place, C?" the head of VAG asked.

His voice sounded scratchy and broken up from the old computer speakers filling the small, dark room with sound. It was the only room in his grandmother's house with any privacy, but the old bitty still did not have cable and the current internet connection was iffy at best.

"Well, I believe so. The execution of my plan will start tonight," C replied.

"And you can't share the details?"

"No. Not yet. But I promise it is good." C giggled and shook his head.

No, he could not reveal his plans. It was a total surprise. No one knew what he was doing inside VAG. C could not risk telling a single soul.

The humans inside VAG did not know about the evil, dirty world of shifters. They could not see the risks or understand their lives were being constantly threatened by a bunch of animals in clothes.

Harrison had his chance to cure the shifter disease, and his poor, disfigured cousin had failed. It was C's turn now. Shifters survived because the world did not know they existed. Well, he would fix that.

C was going to blow the top off the entire thing. And he was going to use America's former sweetheart to do it.

Imagine his surprise when he'd learned *the* Chickee Prinz of his favorite show ever, *Hatched*, was going to be at the CANS this year. They'd announced it in a surprise episode of *The World According to* Marten just hours ago.

He'd had such a crush on the cute little girl, had shared her trials and tribulations as she grew up with the entire world watching her. Oh, he had no siblings, but he had always felt connected to Chickee.

That was the push Clitt, *er*, C needed to really get his plans in motion. It was all perfect now. Yes. Once he had her on his side, C could use her media platform to make every single human in the world see the danger surrounding them every day.

It was a great plan, and he was so close to executing it. Just a few more hours and phase one would begin!

Teee heee teee heee.

7

Chickee adjusted the straps of the silk pantsuit romper she wore for the rehearsal dinner. The hand-tie-dyed ensemble boasted shades of amber and sage that did fabulous things with Chickee's coloring. For a natural blonde, her skin tanned fairly well, and her emerald eyes sparkled beneath the shimmery shadow she'd applied once Dario had finally let her go.

Speaking of her fake fiancé, she stole a glance in his direction, taking a moment to admire him in the resplendent ivory linen suit he wore with a soft blue shirt. It was late spring, and the rehearsal began at five. Chickee had to admit they looked good. Just the right amount of wealthy and self-assured, as if they belonged to that world, and she supposed, in a way, they did.

Dario Marten had been born the son of a tabloid mogul, and Chickee had come from the wrong side of the tracks, from orphaned to infamous, but neither was her choice. It seemed she was always at the mercy of someone else in the beginning. But rich people liked fame, and she was considered a darling of reality TV.

Independence was the most important thing to a woman like her, and it was obvious why. She could never trust the adults around her, the ones who were supposed to have her best interests at heart.

"We should talk," Dario whispered, his large hand touching the bare skin at the small of her back.

That one feature made her fall in love with the outfit the second she'd spied it at Skin Deep. Lucky for her, the designer and owner had several choices in just Chickee's size. She'd gotten a whole slew of clothes for a steal, and she only had to mention the store to the reporters covering the CANS.

"Later. Work first," she whispered, smiling and shaking hands with a few *has-beens* and *never-weres* as she and Dario mingled.

"My God, it's the couple from the plane," he told her, scratching his nose nonchalantly and pointing at the odd couple.

The male was fat and bald. The woman had obviously undergone so much surgery it was hard to look at her. And the man they were talking to— *Well, damn.* Chickee was not sure she wanted to talk to him ever again. Looked like this trip down nightmare lane was going to be bumpier than expected.

Cluckity cluck.

The hallway that led to the ballroom inside the hotel where the CANS were to take place was filled with people wanting to catch glimpses of all the TV darlings. They'd had to pass through a riot of cameras flashing and questions being hurled at them, her favorite of which had been "Hey, Chickee, who's the hunk?"

"Well, I did not expect you to have the gall to show your face here," a deep, familiar voice said.

She looked up into a pair of familiar brown eyes, in an older, more mature face crowned with gray hair. Gabriel Marten was talking to his son, but Chickee took his insult to heart.

"If it isn't the head weasel himself."

"*Tayra*. Hello, Chickee," Gabriel said, his smile wide but not reaching his coal-black eyes. "You are looking bigger than I recall."

"Yes, well, bodies grow from childhood to adulthood. Especially when they aren't being starved by some hack hired by producers peddling diet pills and so-called vitamins to increase metabolism."

"I bet you miss it, Chickee. All the fame. The crowds. Why would you be here otherwise? And with my son. Well, looks like you learned some things from your adoptive mother, after all."

"My mother?"

"Yes, an early conquest, but so clever that little human. Using her body to snag a show to tell the story of her adopted daughter's journey from poor orphaned wretch and single mother's struggle to raise her, to *this*."

Gabriel sneered, looking her over as if she were lower than scum. Chickee was repulsed. Tayra or not, the man was a weasel. And so different from his son. She could hardly see any resemblance at all.

"Do not speak to her like that," Dario hissed, and Chickee glanced to see he was clenching his jaw tight.

Oooh. The man got riled when she was insulted. Her inner hen clucked her approval, and pride filled her at his ready defense.

Sexy protective tayra.

"You know," Gabriel whispered so only they could hear, "I know all about this charade. An agent visited me earlier today, but I admit I did not expect to see you here, son."

"Don't call me that. You shame me with the way you speak to this woman."

"She is a nobody, son. A throwaway. *You* are a *Marten*. I've been waiting for the chance to see you, to invite you back to the fold. Your brothers have all started breeding heirs, and it is your turn to add to our line. Come back home."

"Never, Father. Nothing you say could ever make me want to be like you. I am here because my job requires it, and whether or not you approve, know this. Chickee is important to me. Do not speak to her like that again, or I will not be responsible for my actions," he finished with a sexy snarl added to his accented voice.

Shivers. The man gives me shivers.

"Ah, well," Gabriel continued, "I can see I misjudged the situation. Come. The rehearsal is about to begin. Chickee? If you will follow me."

Chickee turned to Dario, a radiant smile on her face as she leaned up on tiptoes and dropped a kiss on his lips, a simple peck to show her appreciation. She swallowed nervously, aware of the eyes on them both.

"Are you sure you want to do this?" he asked.

"Yes. I'll be fine. It's all old hat, but I wanted to say thank you for what you said. You don't have to fight your father for me."

"Shhh. It is no hardship, Chickee. I assure you."

"Remember our deal," she said, only half teasing. "Don't go falling in love with me."

"I remember," he murmured, running his thumb over her lips and leaning down to kiss her one more time in full view of everyone present.

She heard the *snap snap snap* of photographers, but Chickee was too high on his attention to care. Dario had kissed her stupid.

"I will be here when you are finished."

She nodded, turning around and enjoying the feel of his fingers on her back as he nudged her gently forward. She followed the frowning head of Marten Press, Gabriel Marten, her lover and fake fiancé's father, behind the platform they'd raised to serve as a stage for the CANS.

"Mr. Marten, thank you for bringing her backstage."

"Yes, Russ. Here she is. Good luck, Chickee," Mr. Marten said, but she could tell he did not mean it.

Oh well. He was not her favorite person, either. Chickee shrugged and followed Russ, one of the many assistants, backstage to the room she and a few other announcers were to wait in as they ran through the following evening's program.

"OMG! Chickee Prinz as I live and breathe!"

Chickee turned, wide-eyed, to the sound of her name on a pair of somewhat familiar lips. Wait. She knew that redhead?

"Hannah Bonner?" She screeched the former TV personality's name and allowed herself to get caught up in the woman's robust hug.

"You remember me?"

"Yeah, I mean you were just starting out in reporting when we met, and I was an angry teenager at the end of my career, but, yes, I remember you," Chickee said in a rush.

"Well, gee, I am so glad you are here! It has been too long! And just look at you," the female said, but she did not sound critical or mean like Gabriel Marten when she looked Chickee over from top to bottom. "YOU look GREAT!"

"Who me?"

"Yes, you, girl. You are positively glowing. And I bet I can guess why. Rumor has it you walked in here with Dario, one of the heirs to Marten Press. Wanna comment on that?"

"Comment? Are you still reporting?" Chickee asked, her expression mirroring a deer in headlights.

Hannah had been tenacious back when Chickee was still on *Hatched*. She'd also been somewhat kind and understanding when Chickee had needed a break from the incessant questions and hounding. In fact, of all the reporters from her past, Hannah was probably the one she'd minded the least.

"You know, I am still reporting in my way, but not for any paper. I have a podcast now. And I am not doing sleazy stories anymore, I swear, and if you like, I would love to have you on my show."

"Excuse me, Ms. Prinz is needed on stage now," Russ, the assistant, interrupted.

Chickee could have kissed him. Not that she would. Her lips were currently on loan to one totally hot tayra.

"Excuse me, Hannah. I have to go."

"No worries. We will be in touch," the woman promised.

"Thank you," Chickee told Russ.

"Oh, it's my pleasure. I completely understand. Imagine that woman thinking you would want to be interviewed by her," he scoffed.

"Well, no. I mean she was one of the nicer reporters..."

"Oh, you don't have to pretend with me. I know how it was for you. How it is for you even now. Just look at them, the vultures," Russ huffed, nodding his head at the row of paparazzi likely hired by Marten Press, peering in through the back windows of the place.

Chickee frowned. Really, they should not have any access, but this was how Marten made money. It made sense, even if it made her blood boil. A few rowdier ones slammed their palms on the soundproofed glass, and though she could not hear them, she could see their lips quite well.

Chickee! Chickee!

The press outside screamed her name. Her pulse raced, and Chickee panicked at almost being tossed right back into her past. They really were vultures, and for the second time in her life, they were feasting on her like so much carrion.

"Don't worry, Ms. Prinz. I assure you there will be a bigger story out there soon. Something that will knock everything else off the headlines," Russ said, the gleam in his eyes somewhat unnerving.

"Um, thanks," she replied, moving away from the strange little man when another assistant called her name.

Chickee went through the motions, took her escort's arm and walked to the podium, smile in place. She said her speech, cracked a few jokes, and didn't even choke on her catchphrase when they added it to her lines.

"Remember, don't let 'em ruffle your feathers."

There were lots of mistakes, a few technical glitches, and one very familiar-looking man with dark hair and a ponytail chatting with Dario when they finally finished the run-through. She was so grateful to him for the way he'd stayed and watched all three hours of the rehearsal. He'd looked her right in the eye, bolstering her nerve and giving her focus.

"Chickee," he said, smiling at her as she rushed into his open arms.

He squeezed her tight and tucked her against his side, keeping his warm arm around her chilled shoulders. The stranger offered her a smile and nodded his hello. She smelled fur but could not place his species.

"Wassup there, Chickee? I'm Tony Leeds."

"Oh! You're that PRIC I've heard so much about," she said, covering her mouth when she realized how it sounded.

Dario barked a laugh, and Tony followed, shaking his head.

"Oops, sorry."

"Yeah, that's what my wife says when I catch her calling me that, too," he joked.

"Do you have any news for us?"

"Actually, Chickee, I have news for you, but I think we should talk somewhere more private," the man said and led them to the back of the room.

Gabriel Marten was at the podium, and Chickee felt his eyes on them as he announced the schedule for the following night and invited everyone to the dining room for dinner. He was making a beeline for them, but thankfully, a few other stars needed his attention before he could reach the trio.

"You see, I've spent a good chunk of my career hunting down SCARAB. That's what we PRICs nicknamed the group of assholes responsible for the Shifter Child Abduction Ring and Actual Banishment," Tony explained. "Anyway, after shutting Ranklinger down, we found tons of information in his secret hideout, dating back almost thirty years. Information on kidnap victims."

"What do you mean? Why are you telling me this?"

"Well, Chickee, I don't know how to say this..." Tony muttered, scratching the back of his neck. "Uh, it seems you were kidnapped as a chick and somehow wound up in the system, the *human* system."

"I was kidnapped?"

"It looks that way. We found a record identifying one

Jersey Giant hen female, age six weeks, taken from Virginia on December 18th, 1990."

"I was adopted by Genevieve Prinz February 14th, 1991. She said I was so small I looked like a chicken without any feathers, so she called me Chickee," she whispered as all the implications began to hit her.

"Yeah. We know, Chickee."

"Chickee? Are you all right?" Dario's voice reached her, but she was frozen in shock. Kidnapped? That meant—

"Are they still alive? MY parents?" she asked, not daring to hope.

"We have detectives looking for them now, but the fact is chicken shifters are rare. If there are any flocks left in the northeast, they've been living quietly."

"Oh wow. I don't, uh, I don't know what to say."

"You do not have to say anything, sweetheart. And if you want to leave, we can. Another pair of agents can take over this case while you process this information—" Tony started.

"What? No. I couldn't do that. Um, thank you, Tony. It helps to know I came from somewhere, from someone who might have wanted me. That I wasn't just a throwaway," she whispered.

"No worries, kid. I'll be in touch when I have more news," Tony said, disappearing as quietly as he'd come.

"Fucking shit," Dario growled, pulling her out into the hallway with him.

Cameras snapped, and the flashes temporarily blinded her, but Chickee was kinda used to that treatment. Dario, on the other hand, was a live wire. Anyone got too close and he snagged their camera, stomping it under his foot as he dragged her to a closed-off room. The door clicked behind them, and Dario spun her around to face him, pushing her back against the cold wood portal.

"What are you doing?" she asked, equal parts shocked and turned on.

"Showing you without words that you do matter, Chickee. And you are wanted. Very wanted."

8

Dinner was boring and could have been sawdust for all Dario knew. He was so preoccupied watching Chickee go through the motions. She was stunning, all smiles and charm, and he wondered if the public knew how talented she really was.

For all that *Hatched* was purportedly reality television, much of what aired had been staged. The clips where she'd been duped by his kin, tricked into letting the whole world see her first kiss, first dance, and first heartbreak—all of it was scripted. Most of it had not been run by Chickee. Most had not been filmed with her consent.

She'd been used. And he would be damned if anyone ever used her again. Rage fueled him as he cast his angry eyes on his father, sitting at the head of the table as if he were some great man deserving of honor. The man was a rat. NO. He was worse. He was a weasel. And ultimately, he was unimportant.

Grrrr.

It was one thing to finally discover you had scruples.

Another to learn you were completely devoted and at the beck and call of a single female.

"Don't fall in love with me."

Chickee's words came back to haunt him, but it was already too late for that. He was completely and totally obsessed with the sweet-smelling, hot, huggable little hen. Dario loved everything about her from the top of her blonde head to the bottoms of her pink-polished toes. Chickee Prinz had him. One hundred percent.

She just didn't know it yet. And if he could help it, she wasn't going to. If the only way he could keep her was to pretend he was nonchalant, then he was damn well going to try.

For now, he just had to eat his meal and play the adoring fiancé.

Easy peasy.

∽

"Well, that was painless," he murmured, holding her hand as they walked back to the elevators.

His entire body was wound tightly, like a rubber band about to snap.

"Speak for yourself," she whispered, patting her belly and making a face. "I should have never eaten that shortcake."

"But you said it was your favorite."

"It is, but I have to fit into my gown tomorrow," she said, sighing against the wall of the elevator when the doors closed.

Dario's heart hammered inside his chest. He licked his lips, facing her with his hands on her indented waist. Fuck, he loved her body. So curvy. So lush.

She'd provided the perfect cushion for his pushin' in the shower earlier that afternoon. And if he played his cards right, he'd have her beneath him again, very, very soon.

"You know, I hear sex is a good way to work off a meal or two," he began, teasing the corner of her mouth with a little nip of a kiss.

"Mmmm, is that so?" she asked, sliding her hands up his chest and linking them behind his neck.

"Indeed," he said, kissing the other corner.

Dario bit back his growl when she turned her head to follow him with her lips, searching, seeking his kiss. Not yet. He would not give in so soon. Dario would make her work for it first. He would get her addicted to him, and then maybe she would be more receptive to accepting him for more than just this assignment.

"I would be happy to provide you with such a workout, Ms. Prinz. If you like."

"Hmm, you could, eh? Are you sure you are up for it?" she teased. Her emerald eyes glittered mischievously.

"Oh, I'm up for it, sweetheart. See for yourself," he growled, pressing his hardened length against her soft belly.

The elevator doors opened to their private floor, and Dario smiled against her mouth, lifting her in his arms easy as pie. His pulse was racing and his cock so damn hard that the zipper of his slacks was sure to burst.

Hold it just a few more seconds. At least till we get in the room, he told himself.

A feat made more difficult since Chickee was moaning and writhing, sucking on his neck and pecking at his earlobe. Fuck, but her lips were warm, wet, and so damn kissable. He could imagine the plump pink pillows wrapped around his cock, and the imagery pulled a moan from his lips.

The second he got them inside the room, he headed for the bed, dropping her onto the mattress with a happy little bounce that made her boobs jiggle and a squeak escape her lips. Dario tore off his clothes, stunning his foxy fowl into silence as she watched his Magic Mike striptease. Okay, so he fumbled with his zipper and the buttons on his shirt, literally ripping the entire suit off his body with his tayra's claws to speed up the process.

"Your turn," he growled, his voice thick with his animal.

Chickee's eyes heated as she sat up on her knees, unhooking the straps and removing the belt on the silky confection she wore. It was very pretty. And couture. But not as pretty as Chickee, naked and aroused. Besides, Dario was impatient. So, he took over, pushing her down and sliding the fabric from her supple frame.

"Don't you dare rip this outfit," Chickee hissed as Dario eagerly laved a path from her neck to her belly button with his tongue and lips.

"I won't, sweetheart," he growled, freeing her legs from the uncooperative material. "Are you attached to these as well?" he growled his question, running his hands over the pale gold see-through bra and matching panties she wore.

"No," she moaned, clutching at his shoulders as he lowered himself between her legs and used his teeth to rip the things right off.

"Mine," he snarled, pushing his face into her sex before she could question his slip.

Dario could not help it. She was hot and slick with need. Fuck, she smelled so good, like peaches and her own honeyed nectar. He dipped his tongue inside her heated core, withdrawing to lick her from crack to swollen nubbin.

Chickee whimpered and moaned, her body pulsing around him with every lick and flick of his tongue. He wanted to be inside her so badly, but first, he would bring her to heights untold. He needed to. It was like a biological imperative.

Lick, suck, swirl, dive.

"Dario." She moaned his name, her husky cry music to his ears.

He wanted to take his time, had every intention of it, but once she started tugging on his hair, he knew she was close. Greedy for her, he slid up her body. Positioning himself at her slick entrance, Dario pushed inside just as her orgasm started to ripple and squeeze around him.

She was incredible, amazing, and she deserved another trip into the stratosphere for being such a good little chick. Dario growled, lifting her legs as he reared up onto his knees, draping her thick, perfect thighs over his shoulders. He nuzzled one, giving the other a sexy little nip that drew a pleasured cry from her lips as he started to drive into her, slowly and deeply at first.

Dario worked, steady as he goes, to bring Chickee back to her peak. Her body trembled and her breasts bounced beautifully as he pistoned his hips, harder, faster, creating an earthquake of sensations for both of them, if her yells and cries were any indication.

Fuck knew he felt it.

Quivering and clenching tightly around him, her body welcomed every invasion with a heated embrace. Dario growled, gripping her hips as he lost himself to feeling. Everything he heard, tasted, felt, saw was her. She was his everything. His Chickee. His sweet, sweet Chickee. Her pleasure was the only thing, and he drove for it with every swivel and flex of his hips, until they were both screaming their pleasure.

His fangs elongated, and before he could stop himself,

the tayra inside him took over. Dario turned his head, biting her on the inside of her thigh and claiming her in the heat of passion.

There was going to be hell to pay, but Dario was a proud carrier of the Platinum Dragon card. That was higher than the AMEX Centurion.

He wasn't worried. Right then, he was reveling in the only fact that mattered to the delightfully tuckered-out tayra. The weasel had caught the hen.

Chickee Prinz is mine.

~

"THAT RAT BASTARD. The low-down, ill-mannered, lying, scoundrelly skunk," she muttered as she sat on the toilet seat, legs open, staring at the mark Dario Marten, the motherclucking mustelid, had given her!

"Still a tayra," he mumbled from outside the bathroom door.

He waited a beat, and then he knocked.

"Wanna talk about it?" he asked, sounding sleepy and maybe a little proud of himself.

The jerk.

"No! I do not want to talk to you right now!" Chickee hissed and clucked.

A whirlwind of emotions threatened to topple her sanity, and she could not deal with it just then. She'd had enough surprises today. Chickee had managed to keep her head when revisiting the ghosts of her past, facing down his rotten father plus dealing with the bomb Tony Leeds had dumped on her about her origins. All of that and they were still no closer to finding who was threatening the shifter secret, meaning her one shot at becoming an agent was

84 C.D. GORRI

blowing by and she could not do a thing about it. Then her fake fiancé goes and pulls a stunt like this! Really?

It was too much. She had one rule. Don't fall in love with her. Was that so difficult?

Cluckity cluck cluck.

He was a playboy. It should have been easy! Well, then again, he was not claiming love; he'd just marked her for life. Her inner hen was going berserk, demanding Chickee open the door and peck the shit out of him with her own mating mark.

Sonovachickennugget! BOK BOK BOK!

"Come on, sweetheart. I know I owe you an apology, but I couldn't help it. You're meant to be mine. My tayta has known it since the beginning—"

"No, Dario." She cut him off, yanking open the door. "This was not supposed to happen. I told you. It was a one-off," she growled.

"The first time was a one-off, Chickee. You gave me no restrictions this time." He tried reasoning.

"Really?" she hissed, stalking him toward the door.

"Chickee, be reasonable."

"Reasonable? Oh, I'll show you reasonable," she snarled, seeing the whole room painted in crimson shades of fury.

She clucked and growled as she reached behind him. Finding the door handle, she pulled it open, grabbing his boxers from off the floor and shoving them into his hands before she pushed him into the hall.

Opening her maw, Chickee screamed one final parting shot then slammed it in his stupid, sexy face.

"Go cluck yourself, Dario Marten!"

She was going to have a major freakout now, but the way she saw it, she was entitled. Chickee had worked too hard for this assignment to go so badly. She would not sit there and watch her life spiral out of control because of some overbearing weasel.

Nope. She would simply finish this on her own. Despite her species of shifter, Chickee Prinz was no chicken. She did not need Dario to run interference with the paparazzi, or anyone for that matter.

She did not need him by her side—*even though he looks really, really good there*—at the award ceremony taking place in, *ohmyfuckinggawd*, just a few hours!

Holy Cluck!

Chickee had no time for this. She needed to get some sleep before she faced the mob. Yes, she needed to think, too, but not now. Oh, she would get around to dealing with Dario when she was good and ready and not one second before.

Bok bok bok!

9

Dario wandered down the hall, grateful Chickee had slapped his boxers into his hands before triple-locking the door against him. At least he did not have to walk around bare-assed.

But where was he even going? To the lobby where everyone would see him in all his naked glory? No. That would just bring more attention to Chickee, and the last thing he wanted was for some soulless paparazzi to smear her name across the media.

Again.

"Well, looks like you are in the dog, er, weasel house, son," Gabriel Marten, his father, said from the doorway to the suite at the end of the hall.

It had been years, but the old man looked good. Shifters aged well, after all. The old man sipped from a tumbler of what had to be Gold Bite, the most expensive whiskey offered by a wolf-shifter-run distillery from the neighboring Garden State.

"Come on in, son," Gabriel said.

Grrrr.

Dario did not trust the man as far as he could throw him, but perhaps it would be better to go inside. The elevator dinged in that moment, and Dario locked eyes with a woman pushing a cleaning cart. Her eyes lit up, practically showing dollar signs as she grabbed her cell phone.

Yes. He should go inside. Now. Good thing he was quick. Dario blurred past his dad and closed the door to the old man's suite before the woman could capture an image of him in his briefs.

"The vultures are circling already. This is good!" The old man laughed.

The sound was hollow in Dario's ears, but he'd gone inside anyway. What choice did he have? He took the proffered tumbler of whiskey, identical to his father's, and sipped. Placing the glass on the table, he accepted the robe his father handed him and sat on the couch.

"How can you live with yourself and all the hurt you've caused?" Dario asked, looking at his father for the first time in a long while. Really looking at him.

"I sleep easy at night, son, never you fear. It is natural for our kind. We are tayra shifters, cunning, sly little brawlers. Your grandfather, uncles, brothers, all the males in our line have accepted their roles and taken to them like fish to water or birds to the sky. Only you can't accept your duty," he said and shook his head, sipping from his glass again.

He made a clicking sound behind his teeth. It was the same sound Dario made at times, and he promised himself then not to do it again. He put the glass down and gazed at the man he'd once thought was larger than life. But Gabriel Marten did not look that way anymore. He was older, thinner, a little more wrinkled. For all his wealth, he did not seem happy. And that was perhaps the saddest thing Dario had ever seen.

"But that is where you are wrong. I have accepted my duty, and that is to my mate and to myself."

"Your mate?" Gabriel asked. "But she kicked you out. Hang on. You do not mean Chickee Prinz is your actual—"

"Yes, that's what I mean. I love her, Dad. I never understood how you and my relatives could just flit from female to female, making babies but not forming real attachments to any of them."

"Our strength, Dario, is in our numbers."

"Well, I think you are wrong. My strength comes from my heart, and that little hen holds it in the palm of her hand."

"I see," muttered his father. "I wish I'd known before. Well, never mind. I need some rest before tonight."

"Is it all right if I stay here for a while?" Dario asked, confused as he watched his old man walk to his bedroom door.

"Of course. Despite our differences, you are still my son."

"Goodnight, Pop."

"Goodnight, boy."

∾

CHICKEE SLEPT FITFULLY and for a mere few hours. She woke up with a start, showered, grabbed her wardrobe, and headed to hair and makeup. This was the part she actually kinda missed sometimes.

Not the being unable to decide her style for herself, but, rather, having someone to pamper her. Facials, massages, manicures, and pedicures and having hairstylists and cosmetologists were just some of the perks of being a celebrity, even if only for a day.

"Gurrrrlll." A familiar voice interrupted her thoughts as

she sat in the salon chair. "YOU look like you haven't slept a wink," Hannah said, black-painted eyebrows waggling.

"Morning," Chickee greeted her with a small smile.

"Mmm hmm. So, what happened? Your luscious lover keep you up all night getting your grind on?"

"OMG! Hannah! I am not discussing my sex life with a reporter—"

"Popular podcast host," she corrected.

"Apologies, I meant *podcast host*." Chickee corrected herself and giggled.

"Must be nice, huh? Finally, having someone to call your own? I remember you, Chickee Prinz, a sad little girl who just didn't fit in anywhere. I remember feeling bad about your mama, shoving you into the limelight and feeding you to the wolves. Must have been hard on you, huh?" Hannah asked, a dreamy look in her eyes, and Chickee wondered what was wrong with her.

Chickee gave Hannah a small nod, her smile trembling.

"Sorry, I must look like a dog with a bone, huh? Well, that is because word is a whole gang of Marten Press reporters have been invited by some secret whistleblower who is planning to crash the awards! Don't tell anyone," Hannah gushed.

Bok bok bok!

Chickee's inner hen was going bananas! Hannah was completely human and did not know the half of what she was talking about. But she was right. It was nice to have someone to call her own. That's what the bite mark on her thigh meant, right? Chickee had found her person, or rather, he'd found her.

Dario wasn't what she expected when she'd been paired with the tayra on this assignment. He was considerate, protective, cute as hell, and dynamite in bed, something she knew was more important than people cared to admit.

Viktor's mate, Renee, was the one who'd said it all those years ago when she first discovered she was a shifter and left her old life.

"Will I get a mate too?" young Chickee asked the FUC agents helping her adjust to her new freedom.

"Sure you will," the red fox shifter said.

"How will I know him?"

"Oh, believe me, you'll know when you find your mate, Chickee, 'cause that man will blow your top off. He will know you, understand? Your body will be his happy place and your heart his home. Just you wait, Chickee. Shifters are luckier than humans when it comes to mates because, when we accept ours, we feel it down to our souls."

Bok bok!

After all this time, Chickee finally understood what Renee meant with that little speech. She had found her mate in a man she'd assumed was her enemy. Dario Marten. Her inner chicken fluffed her feathers, spreading her wings inside the metaphysical plane where she waited till Chickee called her to shift. The beastie was more than ready to admit her heart belonged to the tall, text-worthy tayra.

Holy cluck! I love him.

"So, did you hear there's supposed to be something extra happening at the award ceremony tonight? It's supposed to be the biggest thing to hit the tabloids since you quit *Hatched*," Hannah confided, leaning so far over in an attempt to get closer to Chickee that the woman practically spilled out of the hotel salon chair.

"No. What is it about?" Chickee asked, perking up at the news.

"I don't know, but every reporter I know associated with

Marten Press has been tipped off. A few bigwigs even scored tickets for the show," she whispered.

"But I thought it was actors and celebs only."

"Nope. Whoever plans on spilling the tea intends to do it with a carefully procured audience," Hannah added, excitement shining in her eyes.

"Wow. Um, excuse me for a minute, will you, Hannah?"

"Sure."

Chickee nodded and got out of her chair, careful with her still wet nails. She tiptoed to the back of the hotel salon in her paper slides, spying a backdoor. Biting her lip, she pushed it open and saw it connected to a series of back hallways, probably used by staff. Perfect for placing a quick call to Dario.

"Hello?"

"Chickee! Thank God. I am so sorry. I know I bit you without asking. It was foolish and rash, but I love you, Chickee! I swear I will do anything I can to prove it to you—"

"Dario, it's okay. I love you too," she replied.

"You do? Thank fuck, sweetheart. Where are you? I want to see you right now."

"I'm getting my hair and makeup done at the salon. Look, Hannah Bonner let something slip. She said a bunch of Marten Press reporters have been invited by some secret whistleblower about to drop a bomb at the ceremony. I think this could be it!"

"Chickee, are you sure?"

"Yes, whoever this person is, they plan to reveal the shifter secret to the whole world during the ceremony—"

A noise sounded behind her, and Chickee spun around. Uh-oh. She wasn't alone any longer. Her chicken clucked and growled, sensing danger from the stranger—Wait, he looked familiar. It was right on the tip of her tongue.

Bok bok!

"Russ?"

"Oh, Chickee, if you know the secret, then you must be one of them. How unfortunate, and I had such high hopes for you," the assistant she'd met only yesterday with Mr. Marten said, tsking as he stepped out into the faint light.

"Russ, why are you doing this? What do you want?" she said, careful to keep the receiver of the phone tilted out so Dario could hear the conversation.

"I just want everyone to know the world is full of monsters, Chickee Prinz. And I guess I will have to start by showing them you." He grunted and lunged for her.

Chickee dropped her cell phone as she ran down the hallway. The last thing she heard was Dario's angry roar before the madman known as Russ caught up to her, clipping her over the head with his mag light.

Then everything went dark.

10

———

Kicked out of his room, and no Chickee to talk to, Dario moped around his father's suite until he heard the elevator ding. He caught Chickee's emerald gaze before the doors closed, and his heart fell somewhere down around his ankles. He'd ruffled his sweet hen's feathers with his impulsive claiming bite—and not in a very good way.

Grrrr.

His inner tayra was furious with him, and it was all he could do to keep his skin. This was not the place for changing. With a madman on the loose wanting to reveal the shifter secret, Dario had to keep a lid on his furry side. It simply was not safe. Maybe if he spent some time working, he could push his personal problems aside.

Sighing heavily, Dario returned to the bedroom he shared with Chickee. The scent of peaches filled the air, and his chest rumbled with the strength of his growl. Lucky for him, being a member of the weasel family, he did not even need the key card to get inside.

After a quick shower, Dario dressed in his favorite warm-weather tux. The navy blue suit was a unique blend of alpaca wool and linen, especially designed by Eduardo, his personal tailor, to fit Dario's tall, svelte frame. He was not conceited, but knowing you looked good was not the same as being vain. He only hoped Chickee liked it.

A knock sounded at the door, and Dario went to answer it, hoping the foxy fowl had returned to speak to him, though it was hours too early for that. Imagine his disappointment when he was greeted not by his charmingly curvy chicken shifter lover but by a tall, wide bull.

"You Dario Marten?"

"Yes. And you are?"

"Sergio Gravino. Tony Leeds sent me," he grumbled, pushing his way inside.

Dario's eyes widened as he watched the male turn sideways just to fit through the doorway. He was huge. Behind him was a cute little miss with spikey hair and an indulgent smile on her face.

"Hi, I'm Samantha Andrews-Gravino, Sergio's mate."

"I see. Are you here for FUC?"

"Are we here to what?" Sergio bellowed.

"No, dear, he didn't say *to*, he said *for*. Actually, I am currently acting as liaison between PRIC and FUC."

"Ah. So Sergio is a PRIC like Tony?"

"Actually, he's a DIC."

"Um, I'm sorry. He is a dick?" Dario said, though it came out like a question.

"No, not a dick. I'm a DIC. D-I-C," growled the bull, and damn, he got even bigger as his anger increased.

"Look, it was a long night for me. Please, sit down and explain," Dario said, giving up on the idea of seeing Chickee before the ceremony.

No matter. He would make everything up to his sweet-hearted hen later. And if she would not listen to his words, then he would make her listen to his body. Dario had already decided, he was weasel enough to wiggle his way into her good graces, and he was not above using kisses, touches, and licks to seduce her into submission.

That's right. He would simply love on her until she was too weak to fight her feelings for him—and he knew she had them. No woman could come that many times, or so loudly, unless she gave a piece of herself in the process. Chickee Prinz loved him just as much as he loved her. He had to believe that, or he would be utterly useless.

"D-I-C is an acronym for Detective In Charge. Hi, I'm Sammi,," the woman informed him, taking a seat beside her enormous mate.

Dario ignored the fact that the chair beneath Sergio seemed to groan with his weight. He also refused to look at the way the table curved under the area where the behemoth rested his arms.

"Tony brought us up to date on Ms. Prinz's connection to SCARAB. We have news for her, but it can wait until after we apprehend the person threatening our secret."

"I see. Do you have any news for me on that front?"

"Actually," Sammi began, pulling up notes on her tablet, "we've placed a mole in some human groups looking for any hint or evidence of anti-shifter activity, and it seems like we struck pay dirt. An organization known as VAG—"

"VAG? Are you kidding?" Dario snorted.

"No. She's not," Sergio growled.

"Villains Anonymous Group. They keep their identities secret by using only their first initial. Our contact V told us about some suspicious activity involving one of the newer members, C. He's been chatting a lot recently during these VAG sessions about this huge surprise he has that is going to shake the foundation of the world."

"So, this C guy says he has a huge surprise for VAG?" Dario could not help his chuckle.

"I don't see what's funny," Sergio grunted, and Sammi did not look amused.

"Okayyy," Dario replied, clearing his throat. "Do we know anything else about him?"

"No. Only that C is an alias, and he seems connected to this award ceremony somehow."

"Okay. Well, why don't we go down to the ballroom where it is taking place and sweep the room?"

"Can we do that? I mean we don't have tickets," Sammi said.

"Relax. My father is throwing the event. I will get us in."

A few minutes later, Dario, Sergio, and Sammi had weaseled their way past security and into the ballroom where hundreds of chairs had been set up and carpets rolled out. Technicians were busy testing the sound systems and the lights. It was complete chaos, but Dario had a job to do.

His mind kept wandering to Chickee, wondering what she was doing and if she was thinking about him. There were just under ninety minutes left to showtime, and he still had not heard from his heart's delight. Dario checked his phone while Sergio questioned the private security firm, a shifter-run agency called the WPU, *the Wessex Protection Unit*, that his father had hired for the event.

While this was a human awards ceremony, plenty of shifters made up the celebrity roster. It was frightening how dull-witted humans did not catch on, especially when it came to certain talents, like opera singers who held perfect notes longer than anyone else in the world, Olympic swimmers who could hold their breaths for death-defying lengths of time, football players who ran into each other with the force of two trucks colliding. Yes—very odd that humans had not already suspected supernatural creatures walked the earth.

But that was not for Dario to judge. He was a simple tayra, missing his mate, hoping he had not ruined his only shot at happiness.

"Dario?"

"Yes," he said, walking over to where Sammi sat with her tablet and the downloaded list of employees and attendees his father had emailed.

"There are over forty employees with names starting with C. I say we start questioning them."

"All right. I will ask the head of security to round them up."

Dario walked over to where Sergio and a shifter, whose name tag read J. Wessex, stood deep in conversation. He told them Sammi's idea, and Wessex nodded, contacting his team through his earpiece to look for the list Sammi was sending them.

"Now, we can get somewhere," Dario muttered.

A half-hour later and there were ten more C's to go. Ugh. This was boring. but important work. Dario understood that, and yet his brain was elsewhere.

Call Chickee. See what she's up to. Beg forgiveness. Lick her honeypot till she screams for mercy.

The familiar chime sounded, and his pocket buzzed. His cell phone was ringing, and he grabbed it quickly, grinning when he saw her name. Finally!

"Hello?"

"Chickee! Thank God. I am so sorry. I know I bit you without asking. It was foolish and rash, but I love you, Chickee! I swear I will do anything I can to prove it to you."

His heart pounded painfully in his chest, so full it was near to bursting.

"Dario, it's okay. I love you too."

Bark. Bark. BARK!

His inner tayra growled and barked in joy. His mate loved him. He hadn't lost her at all. Thank FUC for bringing them together!

"You do? Thank fuck, sweetheart. Where are you? I want to see you right now."

"I've been getting my hair and makeup done all morning at the salon. Look, Hannah Bonner let something slip. She said a bunch of Marten Press reporters have been invited by some secret whistleblower about to drop a bomb at the ceremony. I think this could be it!"

"Chickee, are you sure?"

"Yes, whoever this person is, they plan to reveal the shifter secret to the whole world during the ceremony."

"Chickee? What is happening?"

He strained to listen, but it was no good. He could not hear anything, just her whispered "rust," but that made no sense. Then he heard the stranger's voice. High-pitched and utterly annoying, the man dared say Dario's mate's name! Anger consumed him, but he held it in check as he listened with Sergio, Sammi, and the security guard at his side.

"Oh, Chickee, if you know the secret, then you must be one of them. How unfortunate, and I had such high hopes for you."

"Russ, why are you doing this? What do you want?"

Okay, so she'd said Russ, not rust. Dario made the correction as he waited for anything else the bastard would let slip about his intentions or where they were.

"I just want everyone to know the world is full of

monsters, Chickee Prinz. And I guess I will have to start by showing them you."

The sound of a loud thud reached his ears, and Dario tossed his head back and yelled his frustration.

"He's got her! We have to find her," Dario said, shaking off Sergio's hand.

The big man had clapped his frying-pan-sized palm over Dario's face to quell the sound of his animalistic rumbling. While he would appreciate it later, right then it was all he could do not to bite him.

"Come on. We can start with the dressing rooms behind the stage," the security guy, Wessex, said.

"Don't worry, Dario. We will find her," Sammi told him, her big eyes filled with concern.

"We better," Dario replied and meant it.

The shifter world was being threatened by a madman, but right then, Dario's only concern was for his mate. It dawned on him then that he wasn't an excellent FUC. Not really. An excellent FUC would care about the fate of the world over any one person. A selfish FUC would let the world burn to save one person. Dario was the latter. He would light the match and set the whole thing on fire to keep Chickee safe.

Even worse, acknowledging that truth did not even bother him. He would sleep well torching the world to protect his foxy little fowl.

Grrrr. Mine.

11

Chickee came to tied to a chair wearing nothing but a paper hospital gown, which meant some pervy bastard had removed her clothing. Her foggy brain supplied the identity of her kidnapper. Russ, the assistant.

"Hello? HELLO!"

"Well, I admit I am disappointed to find the truth about you, Ms. Prinz. I had such high hopes of getting to know you after I shared this secret with the world, but I suppose it is better this way."

"What way? What are you talking about?"

"See this? This serum was sent to me by my cousin, Harrison Greymole. He, too, was afflicted with the shifter disease that plagues you."

"Diseased? Cluck you! I am not diseased, just different," she growled and struggled against her restraints.

"Ah ah. You won't be able to get out of those, Ms. Prinz. Now, this vial contains a serum that will pull your shifter animal forth. Once you have finished changing, I am going to show you to the world. But since I don't know what you are yet, I'll be leaving the room first. And never fear, I have my tranq gun at the ready."

"You BASTARD!" she screamed while Russ injected her with the vile vial.

The effects were immediate, and Chickee felt her skin burning at the injection site. Shit. She'd never wished she had a big, scary beast inside of her before, but for the first time, Chickee mourned the fact she was not a predator.

Feathers peppered her skin as bones cracked, mass dissipated, and flesh stretched and reshaped, going from homosapien to hen in just a minute fifteen seconds.

It took a little longer to shrink from someone her size to a chicken, stop judging!

As she lay panting on the stretcher, Chickee jumped at the sound of Russ re-entering the room. Fucker thought this was going to be easy, did he? Well, there was a reason Mickey Goldmill from the *Rocky* films used chickens to change the ol' Italian Stallion. With a sharp look in her eyes, she waited for Russ to lurch forward, and then she pecked a chunk of flesh from his hand, enjoying his scream of pain as she jumped out of his reach.

The race was on. Stepping out of her clothes and the now too-big shackles, she let loose a gnarly chicken growl. Chickee might be trapped in a room with a lunatic, but she was no fainting hen. She was a motherclucking Jersey Giant —a big-ass breed of chicken, even bigger than her wild cousins because she was a magical one. Not only was she big, with sharp talons and a powerful beak, Chickee was also fast.

Russ cursed as he held his bleeding limb with his other hand, shoving his glass back up his nose. He grabbed his tranq gun and shot a feathered dart at her, but the idiot missed. *Take that*, she clucked, running from corner to corner while the man spun in circles.

"Enough!" someone yelled, but it wasn't Russ.

A new player emerged, a woman Chickee never thought she would see again.

Mom?

Stunned into stillness, Genevieve Prinz stalked over to her in high heels and a tight red dress clinging to her angular bones. She looked awful. Years of alcohol abuse and bad plastic surgery had not treated her kindly.

"I didn't think it would be you in this cage, Chickee. But a deal is a deal," she said, and Chickee heard some notes of sadness in her voice.

Not sad enough though, eh, Mom?

Bok. Bok. BOK!

"Drop her in the cage. Make sure you lock it! Look what she did."

"Yeah, well, that's chickens for ya. When will I get paid?"

"After it goes down, when all is successful," Russ told her mother.

"Chickee?" her mother called to her, but Chickee turned her back, giving her adoptive mom her tail feathers.

She could not believe the feeling of betrayal that washed over her. As if Genevieve Prinz had not hurt her enough in life? This was almost too much to bear.

"I'm sorry, Chickee," the woman whispered before turning back to Russ. "Hey, the big boss says you've got ten minutes till showtime. Good luck."

Russ murmured something illegible as he wrapped his wound with duct tape. Chickee would say she felt bad, but she didn't. Not one iota.

Russ the assistant was a creep. But Genevieve Prinz was dead to Chickee. Chickee would never forgive her mother for this last horrific betrayal. So many people would be hurt by this, and cry as she might for them, Chickee's only thought was for Dario.

Was he safe? Would he flee before the news could hit? She clucking hoped so. But even wishing he would go, Chickee knew he would not leave her.

Trustworthy tayra. Good mate.

All she could do was hope like hell for one last miracle —*FUCN'A.*

~

DARIO RAN from room to room, jostling starlets and game show hosts, pissing off the ceremony coordinators, and giving zero shits about any of it. All he cared about was her. But where was she? And where was that DIC and his FUC mate?

"Dario? What are you doing back here? The show is about to start. You must sit," his father said, approaching him from behind the curtain.

He looked even worse than before. Haggard and old and weak. Dario's eldest brother, Miguel, was with him. His eyes were coal black, like their father's, but flinty like steel, lacking all warmth and kindness.

"Miguel. Dad. I'm looking for Chickee. Have you seen her?"

"No, is she not in her dressing room?" Gabriel asked, concern clouding his eyes.

"She was taken, Dad. Tell me, do you know anything about what is supposed to happen tonight?" Dario asked evasively, noting the humans milling around them.

"No, I told you already, son," Gabriel said, but Miguel huffed an impatient breath.

"Let's go, Pop. Let's find our seats. Dario, you need to leave," Miguel said, and his cheeks were growing ruddy.

"Why? Why do I need to leave?"

"You abandoned us!" Miguel yelled. "Security! Take him away," he said, pointing at Dario just as a ruckus sounded from stage left.

Good thing he'd already met with security and told them everything that was happening. J. Wessex and his team just stood there, waiting for Dario to give them a signal.

"I said, get him out of here!" Miguel yelled again.

"Miguel, Dario, what is happening?" Gabriel Marten held the front of his head, and Dario watched as clarity and focus came and went in his eyes.

"He's been drugged! Call Damon Finn," Dario said, rushing to his father's side.

Miguel tried to shove him off, but he did not budge.

"You know something, Miguel? There is a big difference between fighting Dario, your kid brother, and Dario, the trained FUC. Get your hands off me, or I will show you," he threatened him.

The sound of someone tapping the mic broke the fight before Dario could do more than slug Miguel in the jaw. His brother definitely had it coming. But Dario was still angry as he shoved his brother at the Wessex boys, the security team was apparently all related, and watched Sammi and Sergio get a gurney for his father. Everything was turning to shit, and he still had not found Chickee.

"Ladies and gentlemen, my name is C, and I have come here tonight to show you a monstrosity—"

Dario ran to the stage, eyes bulging as he saw a strange little man wheeling out a table. Oh fucking hell, he could scent her. It was Chickee, and she was scared as hell. He snarled deep in his throat, not bothering to wait. He rushed the sonovabitch who held her. But he was too late.

The madman tore the blanket off the cage where Chickee sat, a two-foot-tall Jersey Giant hen. Her white feathers were speckled with brown, and her beak and claws were both a bright, buttery yellow. She was beautiful and perfect, and the whole damn world was getting an eyeful of her feathery self.

"Here it is! A monster living among us!" the soon-to-be-dead motherclucker shouted.

Dario pushed his legs faster, tackling the madman who'd hurt his mate. The man had his arms behind him as security came to take him away. The crowd was going crazy with whispers and shouts about animal cruelty, and just when Dario was about to lose his shit, rescue came in the form of a tiny, curvy crisis consultant he recognized from FUCN'A.

"Good evening, everyone. My name is Detective Sofia Pelosi, and I apologize for this terrible interruption. This animal rights activist managed to sneak in past security tonight, but rest assured we are bringing in backup, and the night can progress as planned. Apologies again. Oh, the chicken shall be returned to the farm she was taken from. Thank you!"

She waved Dario over, and he smiled at the audience, pushing the cart holding his mate off the stage and to the nearest dressing room. It was so noisy in the hallway Dario could not think at all. He followed Sergio's direction, closing the door behind him as he let Chickee out of the cage.

She was so soft. So cute. He wanted to cuddle her until she stopped shivering, but he needed to see her in her skin.

"I am so happy to meet you, sweet hen, but can I have Chickee now? I need to see my mate," he growled softly.

A minute and a half later, Dario had his arms full of sweet-smelling woman, and he had never been happier.

"Dammit, Chickee, you scared me," he growled, holding her close.

"Me too," she whispered, clinging to him.

"Did you mean it? When you said you loved me too? Did you mean it?" he asked, unable to contain himself.

"You bet I did, you titillating tayra. Now, where're my clothes?"

She grinned, pecking at his mouth with a thousand tiny teasing kisses. Dario growled, cupping his hands behind her neck and sealing his lips over hers. The woman drove him crazy, and Dario loved every second. A knock sounded at the door, and Sammi shoved her hand through, holding a garment bag with Chickee's things.

"She has to go on in fifteen minutes. I'm sorry to interrupt, but it's better for our cover story if she does," Sammi whispered. "Oh, and Sofia wanted me to tell you we have your mother in custody, Chickee. And your brother too, Dario. Seems Genevieve and Miguel were working in cahoots to try to boost sales by revealing the shifter secret. Miguel wanted to get rid of your father as CEO, and Genevieve needed money. It was purely business on her part."

"I was always purely business to her," Chickee replied sadly.

"Hey, she is the one with the problem, Chickee. You were always worth so much more than she ever thought. To me, you are everything, my love," Dario said, holding her close.

"Thank you, Dario," she whispered. "Okay, Sammi, I understand, and I'll be ready. Oh, by the way, thank you. You and Sofia were both brilliant!"

Dario gave her one more lingering kiss then watched her

get ready for her five minutes in the spotlight to announce the CANS for Best Reality TV Newcomer.

"You sure you want to do this? It is perfectly reasonable to be nervous with all the cameras after everything you have been through."

"You make me brave, mate," she whispered, kissing him one more time as they announced her name.

"Tonight, you better make it official," Dario murmured before watching her walk away.

The stunning gown hugged her curves, and Chickee looked every inch the dazzling star she was in his eyes.

So beautiful. So perfect. So mine.

He listened as she read her speech, enjoying the bits that had been added about animal rights and Chickee's own vegan practices. She even made a joke about popcorn that had the entire audience laughing.

Afterward, they sat with the other FUCs and PRICs and watched some of their favorite stars collect awards and have a good time, and Dario was proud of his father's achievements for a minute. Sure, the man was unscrupulous, but sometimes you had to be.

However sleazy his father was, his brother was worse and currently on his way to a prison run by the Furry United Coalition, along with Chickee's adoptive mother and Russe, whose actual name turned out to be the reason for his mental breakdown. But with a name like Clitt R. Russe, Dario could not really blame him.

Hours later, lying in a tangle of sheets and limbs, Dario growled happily, running his fingertips lightly over the still stinging, claiming bite Chickee had given him high on his neck.

"You know, you sure picked a visible spot for this," he said.

"That's right, tough guy. You are mine, and I want the whole shifter world to know it."

"Even though I'm just a weasel?" he teased.

"Tayra," she corrected. "My trustworthy tayra."

"I love you, sweetheart."

"I love you too, mate."

EPILOGUE

"Well, that was a close one," Dario remarked, sitting beside his new mate and across from Alyce Cooper, director of the Furry United Coalition Newbie Academy.

"It certainly was, Mr. Marten. But thanks to our friends at PRIC, I am happy to say the case is closed and our secret is safe."

"Indeed, Ms. Cooper. So, does that mean I'm an agent now?" Chickee asked, biting her lower lip.

Dario squeezed her thigh under the table, grinning at her excitement. She was so damn adorable. Whether in feathers or skin, Dario had never seen anything quite as spectacular as his mate.

Mate. Grrr.

He could not stop saying it. Truth was Dario would never tire of using that word when it came to his foxy fowl. Chickee Prinz was the best thing that ever happened to him, and he wanted the whole world to know, which was why they were getting married in a human ceremony the following weekend.

She even asked his father's paper to cover the event. Her

anger toward the media mogul had dissipated after she'd graciously forgiven him following the ceremony. Turned out Gabriel Marten had allowed his oldest son to be in charge of many of the company's less scrupulous projects, including *Hatched*. Miguel was undergoing extensive psychological testing, but it turned out that tayra was just a weasel. He would be locked up for a very long time.

"Whether or not you become an agent, Ms. Prinz, that is up to you. While we are ready to extend to you an agent position after some formal training at the academy, it seems there's another offer on the table," Ms. Cooper said, surprising them both.

Just then the office door opened and in walked Tony and Sofia Leeds and Sergio and Sammi Andrews-Gravino. The two couples were smiling widely at the pair, and the devil winked at Ms. Cooper before dropping two envelopes on the table in front of Chickee.

"One of those is an offer to work for us."

"You want me to be a PRIC?" Chickee asked, surprised and flattered.

Dario could tell by the slight squeak in her voice. Pride filled him, and he could not wait to witness every one of her reactions as they traversed this magnificent life they had before them.

"We do, and we know it will be a tough choice to leave FUC, but considering your relation to our ongoing SCARAB case, we hope you'll consider joining us. But I'll leave that up to you," the DIC explained.

Tony added, "The other envelope is yours whether or not you take our offer. It's information on a flock that PRIC secretary, Joe the Canary, has found. It seems this is the only Jersey Giant flock in North America. They moved to Tennessee about thirty years ago, after the abduction of their youngest hatchling. Chickee, they want to meet you, but I told them it was up to you. Inside you'll find an address and a phone number whenever you're ready."

Dario smiled, arm wrapped around Chickee as she clapped her hands over her face, tears of joy filling her beautiful emerald eyes.

"Dario? What do you think?"

"I think it is up to you, sweetheart."

"Yeah?"

"Cluck yeah!" He winked.

"Okay, good," she said, exhaling. "Ms. Cooper, I need time to think about your offer. You too, Mr. Leeds. Meanwhile, my mate and I are gonna go to Tennessee. That okay, mate?"

"Yep. Wheels up in twenty," he told her, sending a text to his private pilot.

"You have a jet? Why didn't I know that? And why the hell did we fly commercial to get here?" she asked, shaking her head.

"You never asked," Dario replied and shrugged. "But anything I can do to make you happy or make life better, just tell me, sweetheart. You got a tayra in your corner now, and we make things happen," Dario promised.

"Life is going to be fun with you, isn't it? My own personal paparazzi," Chickee said as everyone stood to leave Ms. Cooper's office.

"Damn straight, my love. Just try to shake me. I'm worse than a tick," he growled, pulling her in for a kiss.

"I love you."

"Me too. Let's fly, chicken little."

Bok. Bok. BOK!

The End...or is it? There are more FUC Academy books from other authors coming your way soon!

To find out more about these books and more, visit worlds.EveLanglais.com or sign up for the EveL Worlds newsletter. If you haven't already downloaded the **free Academy intro** (written by Eve Langlais) make sure you grab it at worlds.evelanglais.com/wordpress/book/fucacademy1!

AN UNOFFICIAL GLOSSARY & ACRONYM APPENDIX

New Jersey Slang

- *Goombahs: Friends/Buddies*
- *En Reponse: In response*
- *Zia (zee-ah): Aunt*
- *Zio (zee-oh): Uncle*
- *Oofa (oo-fah): Emphatic sigh*
- *Nonna (no-na): Grandmother*
- *Impastata (im-pahs-tata): Mixed ricotta cheese*
- *Bruthah:– "Brother" in New Jerseyan*
- *Heeyah:– "Here" in New Jerseyan*
- *Fuhgeddaboudit: How wise guys say "forget about it"*
- *Shawww:– "Sure" in New Jerseyan*
- *Mincha – Damn*

FUC Acronyms

- *FUC: Furry United Coalition (but folks from Jersey call agents FUCs)*
- *FUCN'A: Furry United Coalition Newbie Academy*

- **WANC:** *Working and Administration Networking Core (main building at the Academy)*
- **ARSHOL:** *To the public, the Academy is the Animal Rescue Special House of Learning*
- **ASS:** *Avian Soaring Security (again folks from Jersey call agents ASSes)*

Jersey Sure Acronyms

- **PRIC:** *Private Resourceful Investigative Contractors (detectives are referred to as PRICs)*
- **DIC:** *Detective in Charge*
- **COC:** *Complaints on Campus*
- **HARD:** *Habitable Accords & Resolutions Document*
- **HARDER COC:** *Habitable Accords & Resolution Document En Reponse to a Complaint on Campus form*
- **MMM:** *Maude's Meatless Meals to go is cafeteria food delivered to your dorm or off-campus residence ... called MMM for short (pronounced like mmmm)*
- **HOLE:** *Home Office for Life-Threatening Emergencies (pop-up medical clinics used by multi-organizational task forces during operations)*
- **COOTER:** *Central Office for the Organization of Therapeutic and Essential Remedies*
- **PEEN:** *Physical Examination of External Nuances*

JERSEY SURE SHIFTERS

Chinchilla and and the Devil

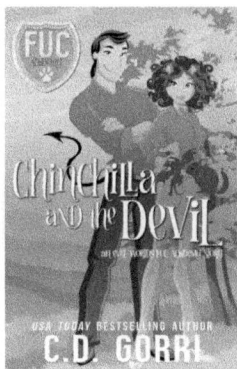

Maude's Meatless Mondays are turning the place into a madhouse!

Someone has been stealing meatless meatballs from the FUCN'A cafeteria and Sofia Pelosi must discover the culprit before the vegetarian cadets' revolt. But she's just an Academy counselor, and she doesn't know where to begin.

Tony Leeds is a private investigator who specializes in locating missing shifters. He's tracked one to FUCN'A but is denied his request to search their records.

When he learns about the campus's meatball bandit, Tony offers to help. He can't resist the curly-haired woman who causes his inner Devil to think naughty thoughts. Will she scratch his back in return?

Buy Now

~

Sammi and the Jersey Bull

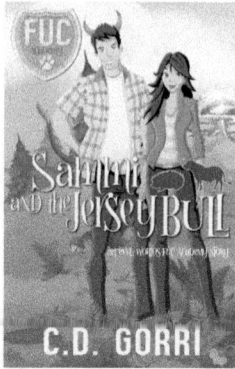

A hedgie charged with identity theft. A bull with questionable familial associations. Tofu Taco Tuesdays are about to get real at FUC Academy.

Samantha Andrews is a FUC agent eager to rise in the ranks. The thing is, she's kinda sorta allergic to violence. In other words, things get prickly when this hedgie sniffs danger, so she's stuck in a desk job at the academy. Acting as a shoulder for new cadets to cry on isn't all it's cracked up to be, and Sammi longs for more, but she isn't prepared for a stranger showing up and accusing her of criminal activity!

Sergio Gravino is just another PRIC visiting the Rockies as far as anyone knows. His real mission is to find the identity thief who has left one shifter brutally injured. Hot on his target's trail, imagine Sergio's shock when his prime suspect turns out to be his mate!

Buy Now

Mouse and the Ball

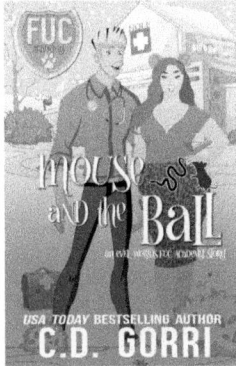

An independent mouse and a ball python with an insatiable urge to protect his main squeeze. Will *Wasabi Wednesdays* prove too hot for these two to handle?

As the youngest of seven sisters and one devil of a brother, Julietta DiCarlo is sick of being told what to do by her older, more annoying siblings. After being rescued from SCARAB, where she was held by a madman who wanted to "cure the shifter disease," Julietta is grateful to be safe. Especially when she meets her mate in one sexy, blond doctor.

Except, *Dr. Hot Stuff* turns out to be just another bossy pants! Tired of being treated to the rough side of Dr. Damon Finn's tongue, Julietta decides it's time for this little mouse to stand up for herself. There's only one place she can accomplish that. *FUC Academy!*

If the ball wants this mouse, he's going to have to prove that he's not another snake in the grass.

Buy Now

ABOUT THE AUTHOR

C.D. Gorri is a *USA Today* bestselling author of paranormal romance and urban fantasy/YA , and creator of the Grazi Kelly Universe. She's always been an avid reader, with a profound love for books and literature. When she's not writing or hanging with my family, she can usually be found with a book in her hand. She lives in her home state of New Jersey, which often features in her work, with her husband, their children, and their dogs, Dash and Chewie.

Learn more at: cdgorri.com
Sign up for her newsletter at: *cdgorri.com/newsletter*

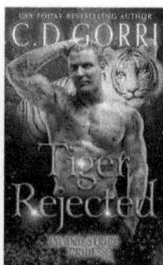

facebook.com/Cdgorribooks

twitter.com/cgor22

instagram.com/cdgorri

bookbub.com/author/c-d-gorri

tiktok.com/@cdgorriauthor

Ingram Content Group UK Ltd.
Milton Keynes UK
UKHW010832190423
420422UK00001B/155

9 798215 353806